Who's TAMING *Who?*

Susan Kohler

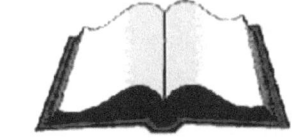

CCB Publishing
British Columbia, Canada

Who's Taming Who?

Copyright ©2010 by Susan Kohler
ISBN-13   978-1-926918-08-2
First Edition

Library and Archives Canada Cataloguing in Publication
Kohler, Susan, 1950-
Who's taming who? / written by Susan Kohler – 1st ed.
ISBN 978-1-926918-08-2
Also available in electronic format.
I. Title.
PS3611.O47W46 2010   813'.6   C2010-905437-7

Original cover art design by Jinger Heaston: www.jingraphix.org

Publisher: CCB Publishing
             British Columbia, Canada
             www.ccbpublishing.com

Dedication

There once was a publisher, Paul
Who really gave it his all,
To approve and remove and even improve
The book, so it sells in the mall.

Prologue

Frank was a happy bachelor, at least he thought he was, right up until the day he met Kate. Oh, it wasn't that he fell instantly in love with Kate, or even in lust with her. They formed an instant friendship, which was lucky because she was already deeply in love. The problem was seeing her so much in love showed him exactly what he was missing.

Kate and Frank were instant friends and bosom buddies from the moment they met in Kate's office. Together, they could create havoc and chaos in spite of Kate's serious romance with the company controller and the fact that they were both hard, dedicated workers. The fateful, almost historic meeting went something like this: As Kate worked at her desk one day, Frank brought her a large, bulky envelope and placed it on her desk.

"Hi! I'm Frank." He entered, eager to see the new girl in the office.

Kate coolly finished writing a sum on her report before she looked up. She saw a very handsome man in his mid-twenties. He was tall and had blonde hair, brown eyes, and a super, friendly smile.

"That's very good, frankness is an important quality in a man," she told him mildly, her face bland. "But who *are* you?"

Frank looked at her, puzzled for a second, then he laughed. "No, Frank's my name."

"So you're not especially frank?" she asked, laughing.

"No, actually I'm more earnest," he said, trying to sound earnest.

"You have a real identity crises there, Ernie." She smiled. "I'm Kate."

"Kate, dainty Kate, the sweetest Kate in all of . . ." Frank tried to stay one step ahead of this clever redhead.

"Cool it, Petruchio," she told him, one eyebrow arched. "This shrew doesn't need taming."

The friendship was on. They were having lunch together one day when Frank wondered aloud, "Why are the good women already taken? You, Laura-" He mentioned the woman who was both the assistant controller and Kate's best friend.

"Because we *are* the good women, you silly man." Kate grinned at him. "Now, if I had just met you before I fell in love with Bob--" She sighed dramatically.

Bob was her boss, also her friend and her lover. He was everything but her husband or her fiancée, a fact that had Kate getting more than a little bit impatient. She reached out and took Frank's hand.

"I'll find you a good woman, someone special." She grinned wickedly. "I think I'll find you a shrew to tame, Petruchio."

"Gee, Kate." Frank shivered as he saw the determined look in her eyes. "Don't go to any trouble just for me."

"Hey buddy," she said with a distinct challenge in her voice, "it'd be no trouble at all. I know Laura will help me. She's a great matchmaker."

Frank almost choked on his iced tea. He knew the record Kate and Laura had for matchmaking. He was wary and also curious. He promised himself he would not fall victim to their scheme.

One evening, a couple of weeks later, as Kate and Bob were getting ready to go to a party she remarked, "Pretty soon, Laura and I have to start working on a solution to Frank's single state." She smiled mysteriously. "I promised to find him a shrew."

"A shrew?" Bob was puzzled. "Why do you want to find him a shrew?"

"So I can watch her tame him, of course, it should be a wonderful match." She sighed dreamily. "He'll put up a good fight. There should be some wild and interesting battles, fire-works all over the place, but no serious injuries, and if we find the right woman, he'll lose, big time."

"I thought you were his friend." Bob was still trying to figure it out.

"Bob, my love, get a move on or we'll be late." As they went to the door she explained it to him. "In the case of love, if he loses the fight, he'll really win the war. You'd better understand that, Darling, or you're in big hairy trouble."

"Yes, Dear. I'm glad you're here to straighten me out," Bob deadpanned, sounding for all the world like a henpecked husband in spite of the fact that he wasn't her husband, yet.

"Darn right, Bozo, my love." She kissed him.

Bob pulled Kate into his arms and kissed her again hungrily. "Do you really want to go to a party now?"

"Of course not." Kate kissed him. "I promise we won't stay long. Laura and I just have to work out a plan for the rest of Frank's life, that's all. We'll come home early enough so that you can have your wicked way with me, I promise."

"The scary part is, I know you mean it." Bob feigned a shiver.

Laura cornered Kate at the party.

"Speaking of Frank, who do we know that's special enough?" Laura asked, looking over the women at the party. "Frank's a great guy."

"And spirited enough," Kate added. "I promised Frank that I'd find him a shrew who would give him a hard time and really put him in his place."

"You're right. Frank needs a woman who can challenge him. That leaves out my first choice, Emily. She's much too sweet and gentle." Laura sighed.

"I've met Emily. She really does deserve someone special, but not Frank. She's not the woman for him," Kate pointed out.

"And you're right, Frank needs a spirited woman who can

stand toe to toe with him in a heated argument." Laura grinned. "And who can keep up with him when the argument's over and it's time to make up."

"Who do you think he would go for then?" Even as she spoke, Kate surveyed the room.

"We'll find somebody." Laura's grin was pure evil. "Somebody special."

Chapter One

Lanie McPherson eyed herself critically in the full length, oval mirror. She had to admit the white linen dress looked spectacular on her, it emphasized her fiery red hair and set off her slender, curvaceous frame perfectly. The dress had a square neckline with a slight gathering between her breasts that hinted at generous cleavage, without being overly obvious. The tapered skirt had a side slit from her knees halfway up her thigh. A wide, bright green belt that matched her eyes and a green ceramic pin in the shape of a four-leaf clover added a touch of color to the outfit. Oh well, she thought, if I have to go to this party at least I'll look good. As usual, she was unaware of how truly beautiful she was.

Lanie hated parties. She especially hated going to a party when she hardly knew any of the other guests, but she felt obligated to attend this party. One of her business partners, Jack Kelsey, was throwing this large party for no apparent reason, and his wife Laura, had personally invited her. In fact, Laura was insistent. Lanie would have begged off even so, but Laura, a very persistent woman, had also called Lanie's younger sister and the two of them set out in earnest to convince her that she had to go. So far, she thought, this whole thing is just a waste of money; with what I spent on this dress I could have bought Cassie a new bike.

Cassie appeared in her bedroom with the uncanny timing of a mind reader. "Aunt Tina's here. She's coming up the stairs." A smile lit up her small, round face. "Gee, Mom, you look really nice."

She plopped down on Lanie's floral print comforter with all the graceless innocence of a child and smiled up at her mother.

Lanie looked down at her nine-year-old daughter with pride and affection.

"Thanks, sweetie. Why don't you run down and tell Aunt Tina I'll be right down," she suggested.

She smiled as Cassie hopped up to deliver the message. Cassie turned around so quickly, her long braided ponytail swung out behind her. Cassie's hair reminded Lanie of hers when she was nine. At that age, like Cassie, her red hair was lighter, more carroty, like a bright red beacon warning the world that one of the feisty McPherson girls was in the area. Now, at twenty-seven, her hair was a deeper, more fiery red; her temper was also deeper, more tamped down inside her, and even more fiery hot when it exploded.

"Too late. I'm here." Tina appeared in the doorway. She eyed Lanie judiciously. "That dress is spectacular and I love the whimsical pin. That color sets off the dress and your hair perfectly, but I'm going to have to help you with your make-up. You are so lucky for a redhead; instead of freckles and pale skin, you have an almost golden complexion that only needs a touch of blush to look perfect. The only other make-up you need is some lipstick and eye make-up."

Tina herself was an ash blond, but she'd received the family's share of the aforementioned freckles and pale skin. Like Lanie she had a curvy figure, but Tina was half a foot taller than her older sister.

"It's the eye make-up I hate," Lanie protested with a grimace.

"I know," Tina told her, "but it brings out the bright green of your eyes."

Tina dragged her into the small, neat bathroom and watched closely while Lanie did her make-up. She picked up a brush and worked on the back of Lanie's long hair, gently tousling the smooth curls Lanie had managed to get her hair into, and then sprayed it again.

"I'm glad Laura called me and we forced you into going to

this party," Tina said. "You don't get out enough Lanie, and I want you to have some fun. I worry about you."

"I'm doing okay for myself. I'm a partner in my own company and I own my own house." She looked around at her small home. "What more do I need?"

She'd scrimped and saved like a miser just to afford even the small house, then saved even more and decorated it to be feminine but not too frilly. The bedroom and small bathroom were both painted a pale peach with floral accents.

"Sure, you have a house and a business but can you cuddle up to a house? Can you make love to a business?" Tina countered. "I'm still worried about you."

"You're not really worried about me, you just want me to meet a man," Lanie told her, "and get married."

Tina looked over her shoulder to see if Cassie was nearby before saying anything, but then she quietly replied with a sparkle in her big blue eyes, "I'd be happy if you just met a man and got laid."

"Tina!" Lanie was shocked.

"Well, I didn't mean it that way, not really. I know you're not cheap. I just meant you need a little romance in your life. Someone to wine you and dine you. Someone to care about you, give you gifts and make you feel special. And, even though you'll never admit it, you need a sex life. Since Cal turned out to be such a rat, you've practically been a nun," Tina continued on in an old familiar theme.

"I'll find someone some day." Lanie defended herself. "Someone who's really worth caring about. Anyway, what about you? You're twenty-five. You should go out and find someone and get married."

"Hey! We're working on you, first. Maybe you'll meet someone at this party," Tina said.

"Maybe. But probably not," Lanie said. "Usually the men at these cocktail parties are just jerks."

"Jerks need love too," Tina laughed. "Maybe even more than real men. Go on! Get to the party. You're already late."

After a short drive, Lanie pulled into the grassy lot next to Laura and Jack's house, barely managing to squeeze her slightly battered gray Reliant wagon into a haphazard space between a red Honda, and a black Jeep Eagle. She took a deep breath and got out of the car. She walked up to the front door of Laura's house, which was wide open, and went in.

Laura's party turned out to be much more than a small cocktail party. It was crowded and loud, already in full swing. It was spread throughout the whole house with an active game of Pictionary in the living room, talking in the family room, and a buffet and live band on the patio. There were plenty of tables and chairs spread around the patio, and dozens of party lights strung up. There was a small area of the deck that some people were using as a dance floor, with the band playing soft rock music, very loudly.

Lanie looked around for her hostess but Laura was busily talking to a group of people Lanie didn't know. She didn't want to join the group of strangers so she poured herself a glass of white wine and found a chair in a quiet corner. Soon a red-haired woman came over to join her.

"Hi! I'm Kate," she introduced herself. "You seem to be here alone. Us redheads should stick together."

"Hi, I'm Lanie, and yes, I am here alone," Lanie replied. "I guess you can tell I'm not exactly a party animal. I was double-teamed into coming. Laura called my sister, Tina, and they both pestered me until I agreed to come."

"Wow! You must be stubborn if Laura had to get help persuading you into something." Kate was surprised. "Very few people can stand up to her."

"Well, you know she only planned this party a few days ago," Lanie admitted, "otherwise, she probably could have persuaded me all by herself."

Just then, Kate caught Laura's eye from across the room. "Excuse me, I have something to attend to. I'll catch up with you later." Kate got up and left.

So there she was after an hour, sipping a glass of white wine and sitting on the sidelines of the party. She had met several men. Most of them were not very interesting, but some of the propositions they made certainly were colorful, to say the least. Do men really think they can just walk over to a woman they don't even know and say those things and get lucky? She couldn't believe it. Bored, she strolled over to get another glass of wine. That's when it happened.

A tall blond man at the bar backed up just as she approached. He turned around suddenly and bumped into her very hard. She felt the wetness on the front of her new dress and looked down to see the stain. It was bright red and it had soaked her dress in the area of her left breast. Without a moment's hesitation, the man grabbed a handful of paper napkins and began to blot at the stain.

In shock, Lanie looked up into the soft brown eyes of the man trying in vain to wipe the stain off the front of her dress. She quickly realized that the stain he was trying to wipe off her dress was mainly on one of her breasts. When he finally looked up and their eyes met, she felt a sharp jolt in the pit of her stomach. The kind of jolt you feel when an elevator quickly and unexpectedly drops a few feet. The sudden jolt shocked her into immediate action. She shrieked with sudden rage as she swung her hand palm open and hard right across his face. The slap made a satisfying crack!

Kate and Laura both gave a little jump as they heard a shriek coming from the side of the yard where the bar was set up. They looked up just in time to see Frank get slapped silly and then yelled at by a short, slender, redhead.

"You great big lumbering oaf! Get your damn hands off me! Why the heck don't you use those big brown eyes if you plan to walk around with a full drink in your hand? It would have to be a bloody Mary!" The woman fumed. "Idiot. Clod. Jerk. You were pretending to be helping me while you were really trying to feel me up. I could tell!"

"You ran into me, you little danger zone, I was standing still." Frank's face was stinging and would never admit that he was in the wrong, not after that slap! "And I never have had to spill something on a woman just to get a chance to touch her breasts, even if she did have fantastic--"

Suddenly his voice trailed off, realizing that he was about to commit a grave tactical error.

Lanie snorted skeptically, a sound that replied to his protests even better than words.

Frank was completely infuriated, his mouth running ahead of his brain. "Lots of women like to have me touching them," he shouted unwisely.

He was so much taller than the unknown woman that he had to lean over to yell in her face. He bent down until he was almost nose to nose with his combative new acquaintance.

"It may be a cliché but there is no accounting for taste," Lanie said coldly. "But keep your great big clumsy hands off of me, if you please."

"And if I don't please?" Frank almost reached for her without knowing why.

Lanie sputtered, too irate to speak.

"Who's that across the patio?" Kate asked. "I just know her name is Lanie."

"Lanie McPherson. She's a friend of Jack's from work. Actually, she just bought into the company and so now she's his business partner," Laura said. Anticipating Kate's next question she continued, "She's single but she has a nine-year-old daughter. She's a fighter. She had been getting a hard time from some of the male landscape architects at the office, so she recently decided to buy into the company. Some of the jerks are going to be real surprised to find out that she's a partner now. Anyway, she's tough enough to fight back."

"Interesting solution to sexual harassment, just buy into the company. It puts her in a position not only to help herself, but also other women in the company. She looks perfect to me," Kate said grinning.

"And they met without our interference," Laura said, returning Kate's grin. "He can't even blame us."

"She'll give him a hard time," Kate said softly. "A real hard time."

They looked at each other, gave each other a high-five and said in unison, "Perfect!"

Bob, Kate's lover, and Laura's husband, Jack, exchanged long-suffering sighs. "Another one bites the dust," Bob said, watching Kate and Laura.

"Poor fool's going to go down fighting all the way," Jack replied, looking over at Frank. "He won't give in without a struggle like you did."

"I was ambushed," Bob replied unabashed. "Kate was naked when we met and she got my interest, um, aroused without any effort." Bob had met Kate at a nude beach, not realizing that Laura had already hired her to work in his accounting department. A coincidence that had made their first day of working together very interesting, to say the least.

"Let's go break up the fight and see if we can rescue her dress. It would have to be white linen," Laura sighed. "It really is a shame, that is one beautiful dress but who wears white linen to a barbecue?"

"It *was* a beautiful dress," Kate said regretfully. "Laura, did you tell her it was a barbecue?"

"No, when I invited her, I hadn't really planned this out. I think I mentioned cocktails," Laura admitted.

She and Kate left their men, went over to interrupt the fight, and separated the combatants.

"Frank, I see you've met Lanie McPherson. She's a partner in Jack's landscaping business. Lanie, this is Frank Morgan. Frank is the head of regional sales with the same company I work for, Lassen-McRoe."

"Pleased to meet you." Frank's tight tone implied he was anything but pleased.

"Likewise." Lanie choked out the single word.

"Come on Lanie, let me get you something else to wear," Laura offered.

"No thanks, Laura," Lanie tried to escape, "I think I'll just go home."

"I really wish you'd stay but even if you leave, you don't want to leave in that dress. I'll take care of the dress before that stain sets in," Laura offered again. "Come on."

Laura took Lanie upstairs and loaned her a very sexy sundress with a low-cut halter-top, bare back and swirling skirt. The dress was a riot of colors; it had flowers of fuchsia, yellow, and peach, and bright green leaves on a black background. Laura took Lanie's white dress into the master bath and gently blotted up as much of the stain as she could from the linen dress.

"My dry cleaner does wonders; I'll drop it off for you tomorrow since I already have some things I need to get done. I noticed you met Frank," Laura said casually as she tried to get the worst of the stain out of Lanie's dress.

"Laura, I know your reputation as a matchmaker so don't even think of it. The man's a clumsy clod and a bad-tempered creep. He was touching me!" Lanie fumed and stomped around the room. "I mean, okay, he's really good-looking, but he's a jerk! He ruined my new white dress and never even thought about giving me an apology."

"Probably because you slapped him before he had a chance to apologize," Laura muttered. She continued, "Okay, okay, I'll find someone else for him. Frank is a very special guy. He's the kind of guy that will always be exasperating, and yet somehow

8

worth it to a woman who loved him. A woman would never be bored around him. In fact, she'd have to be really quick-witted and fast on her feet to even keep up with him. I should have known that he'd be all wrong for you." She watched Lanie's face as the subtle insult landed. "I know lots of nice women who would really love Frank. Some of them are even very beautiful. I wouldn't want to force you to fall in love with him."

"No way, Jose!" Lanie laughed sharply and stalked out of the room. "I refuse to be conned like that. I won't rise to the challenge. I won't take the bait."

"Damn! You would have to be smart enough to see right through me," Laura muttered under her breath.

Lanie would have been even more furious if she had known that at the same moment Kate was issuing another challenge.

Downstairs, Kate had Frank cornered. "Why did Lanie slap you?"

"Well after the drink got spilled--" Frank began.

"After *you* spilled it on her," Kate countered.

"Whatever. Anyway, after it happened, I reacted purely on instinct." Frank looked sheepish.

"What did you do?" Kate asked in the same tone she used on her small son. "Exactly."

"I tried to wipe it off." Frank shrugged. "That's all."

Kate remembered the bright red stain all over Lanie's breast. "You didn't."

"I did," Frank admitted. "It really was an instinctive reaction."

"But I'll bet you enjoyed it." Kate arched a brow at her friend.

"Well, she has got nice firm, round, br--, uh." Frank realized that he should shut up.

"I've got the general idea. So? What do you think? Do you think you could tame that shrew?" Kate threw out the challenge.

"Piece of cake." Frank picked up a cupcake and bit into it

dramatically, then swallowed before continuing, "But why would I want to?"

"Because she's very smart, lively, and good-looking. And she knows how to stand up for herself. You may have noticed that she's even got, um, great breasts." Kate listed her qualities. "But you couldn't handle her, never in a million years. I'd bet on it."

"What do you mean you'd bet on it?" Frank was wary.

"I'd bet that you couldn't make Lanie fall in love with you even if you tried. She hates you," Kate challenged.

"What are you trying to do? Why would you try to get me to make a bet like that with you?" Frank was suspicious.

"Well, it would be a bet I couldn't lose." Kate eyed him speculatively. "You'd never get the girl, I mean, woman."

"But I don't want the girl, woman, whoever. Kate, listen close, in words of one syllable: I do not want the girl. Even I need more than a pair of nice breasts and gorgeous red hair. I have to at least like a woman. So sorry, I don't want to make a bet with you. Especially if in order to win the bet I'd have to win the girl, and I don't even like her, let alone want her." Frank was almost incoherent and practically shouting at Kate. "What kind of guy do you think I am? What kind of woman bets on people anyway?"

"Methinks thou doest protest too much." She shot back, glancing down at his slacks pointedly. "You're lying, she's got your interest aroused. I'm going to change your name from Petruchio to Pinocchio."

"Ouch! I'm wounded." Frank felt himself sinking into a quagmire, a trap. "If I won't make a bet with you, what's next? Will you dare me?"

"I'll even double dare you." She smiled. "Just think about all the interesting things I've dared you to do in some of our infamous office Truth or Dare games."

"Not a double dare! Oh no!" He flushed remembering some of the dares he had taken. "I really should tell Bob what happens in the office when he's not there."

Kate just smiled at him unwaveringly, one eyebrow raised. Frank met her calm, steady gaze for several long moments before he clutched at his chest, finally relenting and admitting defeat. "Okay, I'll take the bet. What are the terms?"

"Loser buys winner lunch once a week for a year," Kate said.

"And what exactly are we betting I can do? Date her? Take her to bed? What?" Frank begged clarification.

"I'm shocked! Any halfway decent man can get a woman to go out to dinner at least once, and I would never, ever bet on a lady's virtue. No, I bet that within one year, you and Lanie will *not* be married to each other," Kate challenged. "Happily."

"But why don't I just give up and buy you lunch every week? I'd rather treat you once a week than be married to that, that . . ." Frank was puzzled.

"Because sooner or later, you competitive macho man, you'll try to win the bet. Sooner or later, you'll realize that you love a challenge and that your pride won't let you give up without a fight. Sooner or later, you'll realize that she intrigues you and drives you crazy. When that happens, I'll have you right where I want you, married to her. You'll be unsettled, upset and never bored, but very, very happy. And I'll treat you to lunch once a week for a year." Kate held out her hand. "Bet?"

"Bet," Frank said, clasping her hand and feeling trapped. He tried one last ploy, "Unless I could bet against myself?"

"No way. You already shook hands on it." She laughed and looked around for Bob. "You're done for, and my work here is finished. I'm gonna grab my old man and blow this popsicle stand."

Lanie reappeared downstairs and Frank walked over to her. "I really want to apologize."

He held out his hand, at the same time looking her over and noticing things he had missed at the previous encounter. She's really good-looking, he thought, short with a knockout figure, red hair, green eyes, great complexion, I may be in trouble, big trouble.

"For what?" Lanie shot back. "Pouring a drink all over my new dress or feeling me up?"

"For both, accidentally spilling a drink on you and instinctively reaching out to blot it up without realizing I was touching your breast," he replied.

"I'll admit you've got great breasts but come on, admit it, you know I really wasn't trying anything. I do not," he emphasized, putting his foot in his mouth again, "have to resort to trickery and childish pranks to touch a woman." He knew he'd made a mistake as soon as he'd said the words.

"You'd have to resort to much more than pranks and trickery to touch this woman," she retorted tersely.

"I've already touched you." He raised his voice.

"Shut up you cretin!" she yelled back. "There are too many people around."

"Lanie, relax," Frank said in a calmer, softer tone. "Nobody cares about our business."

"I care, you stupid jerk." Lanie stomped off totally infuriated, muttering to herself. "I care."

She found her purse and headed for the door still muttering, "I definitely care, just not about him."

Laura appeared at Frank's side. "Aren't you going after her?"

"Why?" Frank was puzzled.

"To really apologize to her, to get to know her, to win the bet, because you're intrigued. Go ahead. Pick a reason, any reason. Just go get her." Laura walked off.

Almost against his own will, Frank headed for the front door. He walked outside and looked around for Lanie. He caught sight of her just in time to see her get into her car.

Chapter Two

Lanie was still fuming as she got into her battered gray Plymouth Reliant. Muttering to herself, she paused and took a few deep breaths trying to calm herself down before fastening her seat belt, then turned the key and tried to start the engine. She was so upset that she flooded the engine. She sat there for a minute, her temper still simmering on high, before trying to start it again. This time the engine turned over and the car started.

She took a few deep breaths, still wanting to settle her nerves before she put the car in gear. Those deep breaths didn't help; she was still far too angry and tense for her own good. She checked her side mirror but it was broken. Damn! When had that happened? She looked over her shoulder, although it was a little hard for her to see out the back of the car because she had so much of her landscaping equipment piled in it. She put the car in reverse and backed up, very slowly.

Maybe it happened because she was still so upset, or maybe it was because the cars were packed in so tightly, maybe it was even because she was distracted by Frank running towards the car and calling out her name. She never knew exactly why it happened, all she knew is that she heard a grinding sound as soon as she moved her car trying to get it out from the jumble of cars parked randomly in the small grassy area.

She immediately stopped the car. For a moment she leaned her forehead against the steering wheel before she took a deep breath and got out. She walked around to the passenger side of her car to check out the damage, only to be met by an extremely irate man. A tall, blond man with angry, brown eyes: Frank.

"You little idiot!" he stormed, just barely noticing exactly who he was yelling at. "What did you want, revenge? You've sure got it. You wrecked my car, my new car!"

"I'm sorry." Lanie looked at his car, a shiny new blue Honda Accord. Then she looked up at him, her irritation and embarrassment warring with a sense of guilt inside her. "I'm really a very good driver. I never have accidents."

"You just did," Frank pointed out with fire in his eyes. "Unless you did that on purpose."

"Really, I'm very sorry." She took a deep breath and tried not to think about her already high insurance rates. Her head was down as she admitted softly, "It's all my fault. Of course, I'll pay to have it fixed. Just get an estimate or two and I'll take care of it."

Once again, she felt that sudden jolt as she raised her head and met his eyes. She noticed that he had a stunned expression on his face. "Really Frank, I've never. . . Is the damage very bad?"

"Bad enough," Frank grumbled. Finally seeing the very real dismay and regret in her face he relented slightly. "Actually, it's just a small dent and a scratch. Do you have insurance?"

"Of course I have insurance!" she bristled. "What kind of idiot do you think I am?"

"A beautiful one," Frank answered absently.

He had, with all single-mindedness of a man who's just seen his new car scratched, forgotten completely about everything else. He caught himself and realized what he'd said just in time.

"I didn't mean that the way it sounded. I don't mean you're any kind of idiot at all, just a very beautiful woman," he amended quickly, "and a very bad driver."

"I am not a bad driver," Lanie carefully enunciated. Totally exasperated she continued, "And I don't see what difference it makes if a creep like you thinks I'm beautiful or not. I could care less. Listen, you jerk, here's what you do: take my phone number, call me later and get my insurance information, give me the amount of the repair estimates, and then forget you ever knew my number."

"Hey spitfire! Where do you get off calling me names? I'm the injured party here! I didn't hit your car; you hit mine. I wasn't the one trying to back out of a tight space with a broken side mirror and my rear window so blocked up with junk that I couldn't see where I'm going. You're not the victim here, I am!" Frank was exasperated himself.

"Well, it makes a pleasant change of pace, don't you think?" Lanie said snidely. "After all, turn about is fair play. Besides, that side mirror wasn't broken when I got here. That happened while I was inside attending the party."

Lanie never noticed the stunned and guilty expression on Frank's face. She handed him a piece of paper, got back into her car and carefully maneuvered out of the small area. She stuck her hand out and gestured rudely at Frank, the old one fingered salute, before she drove away.

Laura came over to stand by Frank.

"Good work." She whispered in his ear, "You already have her phone number. She really seems to hate you but so what? We wouldn't want the bet to be too easy."

"I definitely do not want to win this bet." He scowled, remembering the sharp jolt that seemed to go through him every time his eyes met Lanie's. "That's not just a woman, that's just over five feet of pure trouble on two feet. She flipped me off!"

"Yes, Frank," Laura said sagely, as she started to walk away, "you do want to win the bet." She turned back and said, "I saw the sparks fly when your eyes met, you know. It made the air sizzle. I thought for a minute there was going to be a summer lightning storm."

"You're nuts. Crazy. Bonkers," Frank yelled at her. "I don't know what you're talking about."

"I may be crazy but I'm right," she called back. "I know I'm right. I recognize the symptoms all too well. Remember, Jack makes me sizzle, too."

Lanie got home only to be met by Tina, who instantly questioned her about why she came home wearing a different dress than the one she had on when she left.

"Please tell me something exciting and sexy happened to get you out of the white dress," Tina begged hopefully. "Tell me you did something even slightly depraved."

"I'm sorry Tina, but I just can't. The truth isn't very exciting at all. Some creep at the party spilled a drink on me. The idiot just ran into me with a bloody Mary in his hand. Then the big nitwit blamed me for spilling his drink all over the front of my dress." She fumed, pacing around her small, neat living room. "He even tried to feel me up while he was pretending to wipe off the drink. Then he tried to excuse himself by saying I had nice breasts. To top it all off, he was parked so close to my car that I couldn't possibly get my car out without bumping his. It was just a little scratch but it was a brand new car, so he'll probably sue my pants off!"

"He liked your breasts? Was he cute?" Tina went straight for the bottom line.

"Gorgeous," she sighed before she caught herself. "I mean, I guess he was okay." She gave an exaggerated shrug. "Every time I looked at him I felt really weird though, like a jolt of electricity buzzing around in my stomach and the room seemed to get smaller. I didn't like the feeling very much."

Her voice trailed off until she realized Tina was looking at her with amazed speculation in her eyes. "No, don't even think it. Really. Drop it. He's not my type."

"Your partner, Jack, threw this party?" Tina asked with overstated innocence. "His wife's name is Laura, right?"

"You know damn well what his wife's name is, Tina. You conspired with Laura to get me to that damn party, remember? What are you thinking?" Lanie knew something was up. She could practically see the gears turning in Tina's head. "It had better not be what I think it is. Don't you even dream of calling Laura. I'm warning you. Hell, I'm even begging you. Please."

"I was just wondering if Laura is still the unofficial matchmaker to the western world," Tina mused.

"I think since she and her friend Kate joined forces, the UN finally voted on it and made it official worldwide," Lanie replied sternly, possibly even a little snidely. "And you leave them, both of them, out of this. The guy is a total jerk. He's a gorgeous jerk with a super smile and great buns, but still a total jerk."

"Nonsense, I'll give Laura a call tomorrow," Tina said as she beat a hasty retreat. "Don't give it another thought."

"Why?" Lanie called after her.

"Because you're showing more emotion right now than you ever did with Cassie's father." Tina turned and raised her voice to emphasize her point. "Cal made you hide your feelings, tamper them deep down inside your soul somewhere. Whoever this guy is, he's made you release some of those buried emotions, and he managed it during your very first meeting. You're so angry the room is getting warmer. That's got to mean something. I don't know what, but I bet we find out, real soon."

"But if I've released all those buried emotions as you say, it's only all the negative emotions," Lanie protested. "Frank makes me furious."

"It's a start." Tina turned around and grinned at her. "Besides, at first Cal made you feel wonderful and romantic, then you seemed to just go numb. Look where that led you."

"Yes," Lanie smiled, "it led me to Cassie."

"Maybe I'll call Mom, too," Tina mused.

"Please Tina," Lanie begged, "anything but that. Remember, I'm begging here, do not call in Mom."

"Nonsense," Tina opened the front door, "just leave everything to me." With that she swept out the door. "If Mom thinks she can help fix you up, she might lay off me for a while."

Lanie waited for Frank to call about the damage to his car but he never called. She figured if the damage wasn't too high, she could pay it herself and leave the insurance company out of it. She sighed and thought sadly that Cassie would just have to wait a little longer for a new bike. She told herself that was the only reason she jumped every time the phone rang. She told herself that she wasn't disappointed when it wasn't him.

Several days later, Lanie was running errands all over town. She had a very busy day. She'd bought some new clothes, stopped at the auto repair shop to have her side mirror fixed, shopped for her weekly groceries and picked up her dry cleaning. That's where it happened.

She stepped out from the small, dark dry cleaning shop into the bright afternoon sunlight and was momentarily blinded. She muttered under her breath about lost sunglasses as she paused for a moment to let her eyes adjust to the sharp light. That's when she felt something large and solid crash into her from behind. Whatever it was had bumped her so hard that she lost her balance and her packages dropped on the sidewalk as she struggled to keep herself from falling to the ground.

In spite of her efforts, she fell to her knees on the rough cement. Her dress flew out of her hands and fell straight into the gutter which was filled with muddy, dirty water.

Fortunately, the filmy plastic covering from the dry cleaners saved the dress, for a moment. Unfortunately, the clumsy oaf who had run into her also lost his balance. His arms waving as he tried to prevent himself from losing his balance, he stepped backwards into the gutter. His foot landed right on the dress, grinding it into the muddy water so that in spite of the flimsy protective plastic, the dress was totally ruined.

"I just got that dress cleaned," Lanie moaned as she struggled to her feet. A large hand reached out to help her. That's when she finally spotted the person who had bumped into her. "You. It had to be you. The jerk," she muttered in dismay.

"Hey! Keep going, that sounds like the idea for a song,"

Frank joked weakly, trying to take her mind off her scraped knees and the ruined dress.

"What?" Lanie wasn't thinking of songs or weak jokes at the time. Her scraped knees hurt.

She told herself she wasn't glad to see him. She also told herself that he didn't look ravishing in his faded, tight jeans and soft blue polo shirt. She even told herself that she hadn't noticed his tight, round butt when he turned to pick up the dress, or the intriguing bulge behind his zipper when he turned back to hand it to her, or the flex of his biceps when he helped her to her feet. She lied to herself and, deep inside, she knew it.

"The phrase you used: It had to be you," Frank tried to explain, "it would make a great song."

"It's already a great song, you idiot." Against her will she realized she was struggling not to grin. "And there was also a song in the old days called The Jerk, which fits you to a T."

Frank was so entranced looking at Lanie's silky, tanned legs and tight white shorts, not to mention the way she filled out her hot pink tank top, that he almost forgot where he was. Until he heard a loud honk and he suddenly realized that he was still standing in the gutter with a bus hurling at him. He made a quick move to step out of the mud, but his foot slipped on the muddy plastic. Seeing him start to slip Lanie reached out and grabbed his hands in sheer instinctive reaction. She gave a mighty pull and prevented his fall. The only problem was that when she jerked him so hard, it worked along with the impetus of his forward jump so that he landed flat up against her chest.

Immediately she let go of his hands, only to have them wind up sliding around her waist and up her back. For a long moment they stood there, her hands wedged against his body between their chests, and his hands wrapped tightly around her, stroking her back. They were both breathing heavily and their eyes were locked onto each other's, as if time stood still.

"Let go of me you clumsy oaf!" She finally found her voice,

her strident voice.

"I don't think so," he said, teasing her. "I think I'm going to hold you like this all day. In fact, this could easily become one of my favorite positions unless you pay the price."

"What are you talking about?" she asked, almost against her will. "What price?"

"I'll let you go for--" He paused, thinking. "A kiss now and dinner later." His voice was soft, persuasive.

"Or I could simply start screaming rape and struggling like hell," she countered dryly. "That should get me free from your evil clutches soon enough, especially if there's a cop around."

"You wouldn't do that." He knew it somehow with total certainty. "You're not the type to make false accusations about anyone, not even a jerk like me."

"Okay, you're right," she sighed, defeated but not entirely against her will. "I wouldn't make false accusations even about a total jerk like you."

She had been studying his lips and vaguely wondered how long it had been since she'd last kissed a man, any man. She also wondered what it would be like to kiss this man, with his smart-alecky spirit and that sexy mouth. Her mind was made up in an instant. She thought to herself, what can it hurt? He wants a kiss; well, she'd give him something to remember!

"You get the kiss, but not dinner," she told him with mock severity. "You'll just have to settle for that."

"Dinner, too," Frank tried.

"Don't press your luck, Bub." She thought for another second, then smiled to herself and went into action. "What the heck?"

Sliding her arms around his neck, she kissed him defiantly and with a touch of anger that soon turned into a flare of passion. He'd expected a token, reluctant peck on the cheek; instead he found himself responding to the most explosive kiss he'd ever shared with any woman. She nipped and licked at his warm, firm lips to gain access to his mouth, sliding her tongue in to meet his. She molded herself to his frame, gently grinding against his body. She could feel the solid bulge of his arousal against her body. Her breasts were rubbing up against him, her nipples already tightening into hard nubs.

Soon she was as lost in passion as he was. The noise and people around them faded away and they were alone, in a world apart, in another dimension. The kiss went on and on. People passing on the street stared and made rude remarks.

In spite of his surroundings, Frank was very aroused. Lanie was aware of his arousal, his hardness pressing urgently against her. Suddenly, Lanie broke off the kiss and stepped back. Both of them were breathing heavily.

Grinning, she pointedly looked down at him. She could feel her blush as she said, "It looks like my work here is finished, Tonto. You can have the damn dress; it should look good on you."

With that, she turned and started to storm away. Frank was quicker, however. He reached out and grabbed her by one hand and swung her back to face him.

"You're not leaving me this way," he muttered to her.

"What way?" she asked, feigning innocence.

"Um, uh, all dressed up and no place to go." He wiggled his eyebrows at her before accusing, "Admit it. You teased me, got me all excited, and you did it deliberately!"

"And I enjoyed it!" she added, tossing her head. "Immensely!"

"Immensely. That's not the word I'd use but I'm glad you think so." Frank grinned.

With his free hand he reached down and retrieved the dress. Holding the dripping, muddy garment a safe distance in front of himself, he used it as a shield to hide his aroused condition as he took her other arm and together they walked to her car.

"Lanie, please go out to dinner with me," Frank asked her

softly. "Please give me a chance to just talk with you and get to know you."

"No way." She smiled sadly. "Not now, not ever. Please understand me, there's nothing wrong with you. It's just that you're really just a complication I don't need in my life. Now, please let me leave, I want to go home and put some antibiotics on my knees. Frank, don't call."

"Never?" Frank tried a sad, pleading look.

"Never," she said firmly as she got into the car. "Frank? I know this sounds rude and heartless, and maybe even cold, but please don't call me. I just can't let myself fall for someone like you." She started the battered car and drove away slowly.

Frank was planning his next move even as he watched her drive away. An idea came to him. He had to call Kate, or should it be Laura? Which one would be the best for helping him plan his next meeting with the lovely Lanie?

Suddenly he smiled to himself. I'm a complication? He thought, I'll show her just what a complication is. He was whistling as he got into his car. He stuck his head out the car window as he heard her call out to him.

"Hey, Frank," Lanie shouted to him, "I thought you were going to call me about the damage to your car."

"Lanie, make up your mind," he shouted back, "you just said not to call you. Not ever."

"Good grief! Men are so stupid! I didn't mean don't call about that." She was exasperated. "I owe you for the damages and I intend to pay. I meant don't call me for anything else."

Chapter Three

At the office the next day, Frank made sure he had all his urgent business under control before he went in search of Kate. He found her in her brand new office poring over some month-end accounting reports.

"Hi Kate, you're looking good," he greeted her, looking over her bright print skirt and yellow sleeveless blouse. "I see you've moved up in the world. I'll bet you don't miss your old cubicle one tiny bit."

Kate's new office was large and airy, with pale blue walls and flower lithographs. Her furniture was also new, sleek and comfortable. This office was even big enough for her to have two extra chairs for a visitor. Frank used to have to perch on the corner of her desk when he wanted to talk to her.

"Not a bit. The best part is, I got this new office and a promotion, and no one has even hinted that it's only because I'm sleeping with the boss. Heck, they're all behind me. I even think there's a pool on how soon Bob and I will get married." Kate smiled before asking, "Isn't there?"

"There are three pools about you and Bob, actually," Frank told her, honestly.

"Oh?" It was a question. "Let's see. I can guess at two, but what's the third pool about?"

"One for your engagement, the second one for your marriage." Frank paused, grinning.

"And?" Kate arched a brow and waited.

"And the last one for a baby." Frank's grin grew. "Not only when but also how many." Kate had a set of twins and Bob had two sets of twins in his immediate family.

"Thanks a lot, rat. I have three kids already." She sighed and grinned back at him. "How's the betting going?"

"I'll tell you in exchange for some inside information." At Kate's nod he continued, "All the engagement slots are filled for the next month. Most people have picked marriage slots for about two months away, and the due date for the birth of your first baby, actually twins by popular consensus, is almost exactly nine months to one year away." Frank gazed at her intensely.

At Frank's gaze, she blushed but said nothing.

After a long moment she asked quietly, "Is anyone betting against an engagement? Or against marriage?"

"No, not a soul." Frank grinned. "Who'd be that stupid?"

There was another long break in the conversation.

Finally Frank broke the silence and asked, "What's the big deal with this fancy-schmancy party you and Bob are throwing?"

"Beats me," she told him. "It was supposed to be a family reunion, for his family not mine, but then he added my family and all our friends and everyone from the office to the guest list. He's rented a banquet hall and hired caterers. Now it's totally out of control. The good news is I haven't had to do a thing. He even bought me a dress. A very beautiful dress."

"Come on, Kate, this is Frank. You can tell me. Is this going to turn out to be an engagement party? A secret engagement party?" Frank persisted.

"If it does, it's a secret even to me," Kate told him honestly.

"Would you like it if that's what this is?" Frank asked even though he knew the answer.

"I want to be married to Bob more than anything I can think of," Kate told him. "So if this does turn out to be an engagement party, I'll be the happiest woman alive."

"And if it doesn't?" Frank asked gently.

"I don't know. I would survive but I'd be really disappointed." Kate looked almost sad. "I just don't believe Bob would let me build up my hopes and expectations if he didn't have anything planned. He's not stupid. He knows how I feel, and I know he loves me."

"At least there's hope for you." Frank had a hangdog expression. "Lanie seems to genuinely hate me. She told me not to call her. She even said I'm a complication she doesn't need in her life."

"She called you a complication?" Kate asked, with a hint of laughter in her voice.

"That's what she said. Is that good?" Frank questioned, hearing the amusement in her voice.

"It could be," Kate mused. "If she wasn't interested, in spite of herself, I don't think she'd worry about whether you were a complication or not. You have to matter, at least a little, to be a complication."

"You mean if I've got her worried it's a good sign?" Frank begged for clarification. "Is that one of those things about women and men being from different planets?"

"Forget different planets, try different universes," Kate told him. "Now let me think for a few minutes and see if I can come up with something. I also have some work I need to get done. I'll buzz your office later."

Frank left and Kate got down to business. Later that day she paged Frank. When he answered, she greeted him, "Hey, Romeo."

"What's up?" he asked. "Did you come up with any ideas for me?"

"Come to my office," she ordered.

Soon he appeared in her doorway. "What's the plan?"

"Not so fast, lover-boy, first I want you to agree to do something for me," Kate said firmly. "That's the deal."

"What?" Frank was prepared to bargain.

"I need a spy in the enemy camp, so to speak," Kate said in a dramatic whisper. "The male enemy camp. I want to know exactly what Bob has up his sleeve."

"As much time as you spend with him," Frank quipped, "I thought you'd know what was up either one of his sleeves, not to mention-"

"So don't mention it. Will you spy for me or not?" Kate returned him to the subject at hand.

"Sure. I'll spy for you," Frank agreed, "even if it makes me a traitor to all mankind. Now, what can you do for me?"

"Two things: I can have lunch with Lanie and sound her out. I can uncover her feelings about you, and if there's any particular reason she's holding back on those feelings. I can also offer this suggestion: Remember the dress you ruined?"

"It wasn't my fault," Frank protested. "It was an accident."

"Tell that to the peanut gallery, I was there, remember?" Kate cut in sternly. "I saw you run into her, I saw you ruin her dress, and I saw you get your handsome face slapped. I enjoyed it quite a bit, in fact."

"Okay, I ruined her dress," Frank admitted, "and it looked like a beautiful dress."

"Here." Kate held out a business card

"What should I do with that?" he asked.

"You still have the dress don't you?" she asked, wondering just how dense this particular male specimen could be.

"Oh! I get it." He reached out and took the card. "Thanks Kate."

As he reached the door she asked, "You will get back to me after you speak with Bob, won't you?"

"And you'll tell me what Lanie says about me?" Frank questioned. "Turn about is fair play."

"It's a deal," she agreed.

Kate called Laura to get Lanie's phone number.

"Shouldn't I be the one to sound her out?" Laura asked. "She doesn't really know you, except by reputation."

"But she's more afraid of you and your matchmaking abilities," Kate countered. "Since I am an unknown factor she might underestimate me."

"Not for long," Laura retorted.

"But at least I'll have a temporary advantage." Kate hung up.

That evening she called Lanie. "Hi, this is Kate. We've met a few times and I was at Laura's party."

"Hi Kate," Lanie answered, "what can I do for you?"

"Well, Bob and I are throwing a party this weekend and I want you to come," Kate said openly. "I feel like Bob and I owe you a good party after the disaster at the last one."

"But you hardly know me," Lanie pointed out.

"The minute Laura told me about your solution to the harassment you'd been getting on your job, I wanted to get to know you," Kate admitted. "That was a very brave and smart way to stand up for yourself, not to mention original. So come to the party and we can talk."

"I won't know anyone there," Lanie said.

"Sure you will. Laura and Jack, Bob, myself, and of course Frank," Kate enumerated.

"Are you trying to set me up with Frank?" Lanie asked. "I know you're Laura's matchmaking partner."

"Well, I do think you and Frank would be a great match," Kate admitted freely, "but I would never try to force you into a relationship against your will. Not even with a great guy like Frank."

"Can I believe that?" Lanie asked.

"Sure, trust me," Kate countered.

"Oh my God, you *are* setting me up," Lanie almost yelled. "I've known Laura far too long for you to use that phrase on me. I'm sorry, I can't go to your party."

"At least give me a chance to talk to you face to face," Kate said quickly. "Meet me for lunch tomorrow, my treat."

"Just you and me with no surprise guests?" Lanie asked.

"I promise," Kate said, "not even Laura."

"Okay," Lanie said, "lunch would be fun."

Frank knocked on Kate's office door early the next morning. "How did it go with Lanie?"

"Good morning to you too, Frank," Kate greeted him with a laugh. "It is a lovely day. I'm fine and thank you for asking."

"Yeah. Hi and all that, blah, blah, blah." Frank grinned then demanded, "Now how did it go with Lanie?"

"Well, I couldn't get a commitment out of her to attend my party," Kate said slowly, then she lied, "but she is meeting me for lunch the day after tomorrow."

"That's great!" Frank grinned. "Maybe you'll find out why she's avoiding me."

"The reason for that may be simple." Kate pointed out, "She may just plain not like you."

"I know it's possible but I don't think so," Frank said firmly.

"Gee, Frank, no conceit there!" Kate shot back at him. "Talk about a male ego."

"That's not how I meant it." Frank recalled, "That kiss sure didn't feel like dislike to me."

"Well, I'll find out what's up and get her to the party. The rest of it is up to you." Kate changed the subject. "Now enough about you, what's up with Bob and this party?"

"I'm sorry to report that I failed in my mission," Frank said formally. "I was sloppy and got caught."

"Caught?" Kate queried.

"Bob knew I was spying for you the minute I walked into his office," Frank admitted. Then he became indignant and continued, "He said to tell you, and I quote, 'You'll need someone a lot smarter and trickier than Frank to get secrets out of me,' and then he told me to get back to work! Can you imagine?"

"Frank! Where did I go wrong? I thought I had trained you better than that!" Kate chided, sounding very disappointed in him. "I'll have to send you to remedial spy school."

"I'm so ashamed." Frank pretended to sob. "I do know one

thing though. Something is definitely up. He has got something planned for the party. I don't know what, but he has got a plan. If I had to guess, I'd say a proposal."

"Which I'd accept," Kate murmured.

"Oh, really?" Frank tried to act surprised.

"Oh, definitely really." Kate sounded dreamy.

The next day Kate met Lanie for lunch. In spite of her lie to Frank about just when this lunch was taking place, she kept one eye open as she drove to the restaurant. She realized that if Frank knew she was meeting Lanie, he would try to follow her. She has dressed for casual comfort in a floral skirt, T-shirt and sandals. Lanie, as a landscaper, worked almost everyday in shorts and a T-shirt. She joined Kate at a local buffet. After hitting the salad bar both women sat down to talk.

"First thing I want to say, Lanie, is that whether or not there is the slightest chance that you will ever give Frank a shot, I want us to become friends," Kate told Lanie. "From what Laura's told me about you, I think we can become good pals."

"I get that feeling too," Lanie admitted, "as long as you don't push me into a wild romance with some overgrown Romeo who would never commit to a real life together."

"If you mean Frank," Kate told her, "you're wrong about him. He is definitely one of the good guys. He's a little crazy and he loves to joke around but he would commit in a minute, and once he committed he would be completely faithful to the right woman. He would also manage to keep her exasperated and off-balance, yet still treat her like a queen."

"If only he wasn't such a jerk," Lanie sighed.

"But I'll bet he kisses good," Kate said in an offhand manner.

"That's one bet you'd win." Lanie blushed.

"Funny, he said the same thing about you." Kate finished her salad. "Let's get some dessert."

"All you've had is salad, aren't you going to eat a main course?" Lanie quizzed.

"Maybe later, after dessert," Kate told her grinning. "Hey, we're moms. We're the ones who set the rules. Who says we have to follow them while the kids aren't here?"

"Good point." Lanie laughed. "Isn't hot fudge one of the basic food groups?"

"Don't tell my kids but I've always thought it was." Kate smiled with a memory. "Remind me to tell you sometime just exactly what Bob can do with hot fudge."

"I'll bet I can guess." Lanie grinned. "I can tell you're really happy with Bob. I don't think I've ever been in love myself, not like that."

"All the more reason you should stop fighting and give Frank a chance," Kate pointed out. "He might just be the one."

"There's not only me to think of, I have Cassie," Lanie replied thoughtfully. "I can't let her get hurt."

"Frank is terrific with my kids. I trust him to babysit, and they love him like an uncle," Kate told her. "And I have three, all under five years old, and six dogs."

"Six dogs?"

"Well, a pair and four puppies," Kate clarified. "But between them and the three kids, Frank will still volunteer to babysit, and I've *never* come home to a mess. Now that's a good man."

"I didn't know you had kids," Lanie told her, "until you mentioned being a mom a few minutes ago."

"Boy, am I a mom. I have three, a boy five and twin girls, just about to turn two," Kate told her. "I'm also a widow."

"Whoa! That's tragic. I'm so sorry to think of you going through something like that," Lanie said sadly. "Losing someone you love and being left with three small children to care for… I can't even begin to imagine how terrible it must have been for you. It's amazing to see you so happy now."

"Well, I found Bob with Laura's help, of course." Kate told her firmly, "You could be that happy, too. You deserve it as much as anyone I've met lately. So, are you going to come to my party?"

"What will you do if I say no?" Lanie asked. "Would you do what Laura did and call in my sister to help persuade me to go?"

"Nah," Kate said with a shrug, "I'd skip the little stuff and bring in the big guns, so to speak."

"You don't mean-" Lanie looked shocked.

"Yep." Kate looked lethal. "I'd call in your mom. Laura said she was relentless."

"You are really ruthless." Lanie shook her head. "I thought you might be less persistent than Laura but you're even worse."

"You'd better believe it; I have to be to keep up with her." Kate softened her tone. "Lanie, will you please come to my party?"

"Yes." She smiled. "I know when I'm outgunned."

"It's only because we want to see you happy. Please come. Promise?" Kate prompted.

"Yes," Lanie said softly, "but please, don't throw Frank at me."

"No throwing," Kate promised with her fingers crossed, "just be there, and give him a fair chance."

"He is kinda cute, isn't he?" Lanie relented.

"And he's trainable, he has real potential," Kate agreed.

"Well, I guess I'll get a sitter for Cassie and be there," Lanie said softly.

"Sitter?" Kate said questioningly. "Are you nuts? Bring Cassie."

"To a formal party?" Lanie puzzled.

"Of course. Look, my kids will be there, and Bob's nieces and nephews, *all* of Bob's nieces and nephews, and several of the guests are bringing their kids." Kate explained, "Bob's even rented a room close to the banquet hall with a sitter in case any of the kids get tired or bored at the party. They'll have toys, videos and special food, and of course video games."

"All right, we'll be there." Lanie smiled. "Cassie will love it."

"I hope she does." Kate smiled softly. "I hope I do, too."

"What do you mean?" Lanie asked.

"I'm hoping this turns out to be an engagement party," Kate said, "for Bob and me."

"Well, you're a take-charge kind of woman. Make it one," Lanie suggested. "If he doesn't ask you, ask him."

"Hey! You're right." Kate smiled. "Oh my gosh! Look at the time! Sorry Lanie but I have to get back to work." The two women parted.

"Frank, can you come into my office, please? When it's convenient," Kate said into the intercom.

Frank came in and sat in one of the comfortable chairs across from her desk. "What's up?"

"I lied to you," Kate admitted. "I said I was going to lunch with Lanie tomorrow but we had lunch together today instead."

"Why?" Frank was puzzled.

"So you wouldn't try to follow us and sabotage my best efforts," Kate returned.

"And how did it go?" Frank wanted to get to the point.

"She'll be at the party with her daughter," Kate said, "and I promised not to throw you at her, so you're on your own."

"I'm up to it," Frank insisted.

"I do have a suggestion though," Kate added. "Get her daughter to like you. Lanie's a very loving and protective mom."

"I'm good with kids, you know that," Frank said proudly. "And I really like kids, even if I'm not interested in their moms."

"But this little girl is important," Kate said, "and Lanie is smart enough to spot it if your friendship to the girl is even slightly phony or forced."

"Kate, give me some credit." Frank left in a feisty mood but came back a minute later just to stick his head in the door and say, "Thanks."

Chapter Four

Lanie was among the last of the guests to arrive at Kate and Bob's fancy and mysterious party. She looked stunning. She was wearing an emerald green dress with a soft, velvet bodice trimmed with sequins beads, and a full swirling skirt made of chiffon. The dress had spaghetti straps and a low, square neckline. A brightly beaded, multicolored jacket with lots of emerald green in the beading completed the outfit. The color of the dress set off her hair and complexion perfectly.

She had Cassie at her side, holding her hand. Cassie was in a frilly dress, the color of rich wine, with a lace collar and lace cuffs. She had on shiny black shoes with white stockings. She looked very pretty and excited.

Almost the first person Lanie spotted across the room was Frank. He was in a charcoal gray suit, and he looked fantastic. He turned to look at the door just as Lanie entered the room and the look in his eyes stunned her. He didn't smile or move at all. He just looked at her with a peculiar expression in his eyes. He looked – she tried to think of a word, and then suddenly it hit her – he looked ravenous. She was stunned when the right word hit her, frozen to the spot. Before she could react Kate came over to greet her.

"I'm so glad you came. Here's some champagne for you and some cider for your daughter," Kate greeted Lanie. She handed her a flute of champagne and an identical champagne flute filled with sparkling cider to Cassie.

Lanie returned the greeting. Then Kate turned her attention to Lanie's daughter. "This must be Cassie. She's beautiful. Hi Cassie, I'm Kate."

"Hi Kate. Thank you for letting me come to your party with my Mom," Cassie said.

"I'm glad you're here, the party wouldn't be the same without you," Kate told the girl.

Lanie looked Kate over. "You look radiant and also a bit anxious. Have you found out what Bob's planning yet?"

"No," Kate grinned, "unless he's planning to drive me nuts, and he's already succeeded at that."

"You'll find out what's up pretty soon." Lanie smiled. "I'm betting you'll be very happy before the night's over."

"I hope you're right. Now go greet Frank while I take Cassie and introduce her to some of the other kids." Kate pointed to a side door. "We have a special room for them with a sitter, Suite 101, and some special treats including video games and a few other surprises."

"Okay, she can go. I won't promise to go over to Frank, though he can come to me." Lanie smiled at Cassie. "Go have fun, Sweetie. I'll be here if you need me."

Frank was still standing there watching her, but she didn't get a chance to decide whether to go over and meet him. As soon as Kate and Cassie were gone, Laura and Jack came over. They brought Bob along and introduced him to Lanie.

"I understand Kate and Laura are trying to play matchmaker with your life," he told her with a great deal of sympathy. "You have no idea how far those two will go. The saving grace is that they only want to see you and Frank happy. This whole party is a direct result of Laura's matchmaking."

"So? I have gotten their special treatment. How did I get so lucky?" Lanie asked, sipping her champagne. "Neither one of them really knows me all that well."

"I think it was Frank they were working on." Bob smiled. Then, distracted by his own nerves and perhaps a glass or two of champagne, he put his foot well and truly into his mouth. "All I know is that Kate promised to find Frank a shre-" He shut up very abruptly.

Laura shot him a look that could melt steel. Jack whispered, "Better you than me," under his breath, then abruptly walked over to the other side of the room.

Bob looked after him and muttered, "Coward," very softly.

Lanie looked back and forth from Laura to Bob, puzzled. "Kate promised to find Frank a what?"

"It was just a joke she made before she ever met you, before you ever met Frank. Please don't get insulted," Laura said quickly, "it really didn't have anything to do with you as a person."

"A what?" Lanie was more demanding. "Kate promised to find Frank a what?"

"A shrew," Laura answered softly. "Kate only said it because Frank quoted a few lines from *The Taming of the Shrew* when they first met."

"I am not a shrew!" Lanie defended herself. "Am I?"

"Of course not." Laura led her to a chair. "And we don't expect Frank to tame you either. That would be insulting and get us thrown out of the sisterhood. We were hoping to find him a fantastic woman with enough fire and spirit to tame *him*. Of course, we just couldn't tell him that. He's only a man."

"Of course not," Lanie conceded.

"The thing that made us think you would be perfect for him was the way you slapped him at my party." Laura smiled. "And the way your eyes were shooting sparks as you stood up to him."

"You mean this all started because we fought at your party?" Lanie was surprised.

"It was a great fight," Laura said, "but that's not all. Lanie, there were sparks flying between you two, and not all of them were caused by anger. Both of us noticed it."

"Maybe not all of the sparks were anger," Lanie relented, "just most of them."

"So go over and talk to him." Laura grinned. "Give him a

hard time. What can it hurt? I have to find Kate."

The room seemed three miles wide as Lanie walked towards Frank. He met her halfway across the room. Without a word, he took the almost full champagne glass from her hand and set it on the nearest table. Then he led her to the dance floor and took her into his arms.

As she started to say something, a protest perhaps, Frank brushed his fingers over her mouth softly, tracing her lips with his forefinger.

"Let's have at least one romantic dance before we start arguing. Please," he said softly. "We can start a new tradition."

Her breath seemed to stick in her throat so she only nodded. She snuggled against him as they moved to the slow, romantic music. They managed two full songs before the haze cleared and they began to make small talk.

They continued to dance as they discussed the party. "Frank, do you know what the occasion is? This is no ordinary family reunion."

"I'm hoping for Kate's sake that Bob means to propose and turn this into an engagement party," he told her. "I tried to sound him out for Kate but he knew I was spying."

"Well, I talked to Kate about it," Lanie said, "and if he doesn't ask her to marry him, she'll ask him to marry her."

"Good for her!" Frank grinned. "She's loved him from the moment they met."

"It must be wonderful to love and be loved like that." Lanie sounded dreamy.

"It is," Frank agreed, "if you open yourself up to that kind of love. That means being willing to risk heartache."

"I'm willing to risk heartache," Lanie defended herself, "for myself, but not for Cassie."

"I can understand how that would worry you," Frank swung her around to the music, "but it can't stop you from living."

"Do you think I use Cassie to close myself off from life?"

Lanie quizzed. "Is that what you mean?"

"I'm not sure. To be truthful, I don't think anyone can answer that question for you." Frank murmured, "But I think it's possible. It's something to consider."

"Okay, I'll think about it," Lanie agreed. "Meanwhile, would you like to meet Cassie?"

"Yes, I would, very much." Frank smiled at her. "I saw you as you entered the room with her, she looked beautiful. You, by the way are heart stopping, breathtaking, and all that jazz."

"Thank you, kind sir." Lanie grinned. "You're not looking too bad yourself."

They walked to the kid's room to get Cassie. She greeted them excitedly. "Mommy, they have puppies!"

She gently held a soft furry Boston Terrier puppy in her hands. It squirmed and made soft puppy sounds. Lanie admired the little puppy for a moment before she had Cassie put it back with its mother.

Together the three of them walked over to an empty table at the far end of the room. They sat and talked together. Frank, Lanie noticed, was very good with Cassie. He didn't talk down to her like she was a subhuman instead of a child. He also didn't try too hard by going out of his way to ingratiate himself with her. It was a good thing, too. Cassie was sharp; she would have spotted any artificial attempts at friendship in a minute.

Finally Cassie asked, "Are you the man who spilled tomato juice all over Mommy's white linen dress?"

"Yes, I am," Frank admitted. "It was an accident."

"Was it really?" Cassie asked wide-eyed. "Aunt Tina said so but Mommy said you were only trying to feel her up. Whatever that means."

"Your Aunt was right," Frank said slowly, "but when I tried to blot up the tomato juice, I touched your Mommy where I shouldn't have. Accidentally, it wasn't on purpose."

"That makes sense to me," Cassie decided. "After all, you

couldn't control where the juice went."

"I'm glad you understand because your Mommy didn't." Frank grinned at the girl. "She was very mad at me."

"She was just upset." Cassie explained, "That was a new dress. She said it cost an arm and a leg."

"I'm sorry I got so mad at you, Frank," Lanie said softly.

"Forget it," Frank turned to smile at her, "anyone would have been upset."

"But still-" Lanie began, but she was stopped by Bob who was at the bandstand making an announcement.

"Excuse me, everybody. May I have your attention?" Bob waited for the guests to settle down and look up at him. "I have two things to tell you: The first one probably won't surprise any of you. Kate has accepted my proposal of marriage." He paused for a long moment to let the group react with catcalls, applause and good wishes. "Wait! There's more." He held up his hand to stop the guests from rushing up to the stage to congratulate them.

Bob went back to the microphone. "The second announcement may actually surprise you. It surprised Kate." He grinned at Kate who gave him a companionable but slightly off-kilter grin in return. "The second announcement is that the wedding is going to take place right here and now. Jeff, I need you to act as my Best Man."

There was a surprised murmur from all of the party guests. The hotel staff got busy opening a partition and expanding the banquet room, revealing that it had another dais surrounded by flowers. They had chairs lined up in front of the dais. There was an aisle down the center of the group of chairs with a long red carpet. Stretching from the first row to the last, the chairs lining the aisle had a long garland of white ribbons and pale roses that matched Kate's dress.

Everyone stared in amazement as they saw the banquet staff wheel over a small table near the buffet. It contained a four-tiered wedding cake with forks and plates. The guests were invited to seat themselves.

"Did you know anything about this?" Lanie asked Frank.

"I didn't have a hint." Frank pointed out, "Look at Bob's brother Jeff, the Best Man, even he's in a state of shock."

"Kate must be thrilled," Lanie said, smiling widely.

"Kate looks like she's in shell shock." Frank laughed.

It was a beautiful wedding, both lovely and touching. There was even quite a bit of humor mixed in with the formality. Not only did the two little flower girls pelt the wedding guests with rose petals, but Laura, as the Matron of Honor and the Best Man each had an adult Boston Terrier beside them. The Best Man's dog was sporting a white collar and a black tie, and Laura's dog had roses fastened to her collar.

Kate was radiant in her soft tangerine dress with its full chiffon skirt and beaded bodice. Her father, resplendent in a formal tuxedo, walked beside her up the aisle.

"Dearly beloved," the Minister began, "I see we have the whole family here, including the four-legged members of the family, and friends. We have gathered together . . ."

It was touching and beautiful. As they partied afterwards, Lanie and Frank both got a little tipsy on the champagne. During the reception, Kate and Bob made their way around the room. When they got to the table with Lanie, Frank and Cassie, they stopped to talk.

"Cassie, you're just the person I wanted to see," Kate said. "I'd really like someone to hold this dog for me. In fact, if you want, you can take her back to the room where the kids are. We have the rest of the puppies in there. They're also serving a special wedding cake in there."

"Mommy, can I go?" Cassie asked as she held the leash very carefully. "I want to play with the puppies again."

"Yes, love," Lanie told her daughter, "have fun."

Lanie watched for a minute as her daughter left before she

turned to hug Kate. "Congratulations!"

"Thanks," Kate said, tears in her eyes.

Lanie and Frank both took turns hugging and congratulating Bob before he left. He had to find someone special and ask her to dance. After he left, Kate explained, "He wants to dance with Ida, my former mother-in-law. It's his way of letting her know that she is still part of this family."

"That's so sweet," Lanie said, "and very thoughtful. This wedding however was more than thoughtful, it was stunning. He really planned this whole thing before even proposing? You really didn't know anything about it?"

"Not a clue," Kate said. "I should have though."

"Why, Kate?" Frank inquired.

"Because, after our houses were vandalized, remember Frank?" At his nod she continued, "Bob asked me about my wedding with Joe." She said thoughtfully, "I told him the planning drove me crazy and took some of the fun out of the day because I was so scared something would go wrong. I wanted everything to be perfect. That handsome devil gave me just what I wanted, a beautiful wedding with no stressful planning!"

"It took a lot of nerve on his part, planning and setting all of this up when he hadn't even asked you to marry him," Lanie said softly.

"It's called love, Lanie, give it a chance." Kate kissed her cheek. "I'd better go mingle or else they'll start demanding we have one of those dreary receiving lines."

Kate hugged and kissed Frank and whispered rather carelessly, "You're winning."

"What did that mean?" Lanie asked.

"Oh, nothing." Frank was lying and Lanie saw it the moment the words were out of his mouth.

A short time later, near the punch bowl, the seemingly inevitable happened. One of the many children at the party bumped into Frank, who sidestepped quickly but bumped into Lanie, spilling champagne down the front of her dress. Frank grabbed a handful of napkins and started to blot Lanie's dress but he took one look at her face and silently handed her the napkins.

Finally he spoke. "Sorry. Why aren't you yelling at me?"

Lanie smiled at him. "For one thing, it wasn't your fault. Plus, I had the dress treated with a protective coating against stains."

Just then, Laura and her slightly tipsy husband, Jack came over. Jack saw the wet spot on the front of Lanie's dress and said, "My God! Frank, if you keep that up, you'll never win the bet."

It was the second reference to winning she'd heard, and Lanie wasn't a stupid woman. "What bet?"

"Lanie, please don't get upset, it was only a joke." Laura tried to calm the situation. "Jack just has a big mouth, which is going to cost him plenty when we get home."

"Leave us please," Frank said to Laura and Jack.

After they left, Frank took Lanie by the arm and firmly led her out the side doors and into a garden. He found a private spot. He sat on a bench and pulled her down beside him.

"It was just a trick Kate played on me, to get me to take a second look at you," Frank explained. "I was angry when we met, and she bet me that I couldn't win you."

"Win me how?" Lanie asked, suspicion and incipient wrath warred within her. "What was the wager?" Were you just supposed to date me or did you have to get me in bed? What?"

"It was to marry you," Frank said, exasperated. "We would never bet on bedding you, that would be rotten!"

"And what would you have won?" Lanie asked very quietly.

"Lunch once a week for a year," Frank admitted.

"And what do you think you're going to get now," Lanie asked.

"I think I'm going to get my head handed to me on a platter," Frank said, almost whining. "And it's not fair, that bet didn't mean anything. It was just a way for Kate to get me to notice you. Believe me Lanie, if I wasn't really interested in you, I wouldn't be around you."

"Believe you?" Lanie shrieked, and the fight was on. "You're a lowlife cad who bets on a woman's future, why should I believe you?"

They argued back and forth for several minutes before Frank scored a direct hit to her ego. "Lanie, you're being ridiculous! Do you really think I would marry a woman just so that Kate would buy my lunch once a week? I know you don't! You're just a coward who's using this bet to keep me at a distance. I was finally getting close to you and that has you in a panic."

"Coward! In a panic, am I?" She was so angry she was developing a Scottish burr, even though she was third generation American. "Well Frank, let me just say this in very simple words even you can understand. I don't want to see you, I don't want you to call me, email me or contact me in any way. Just leave me alone. Got it?"

She knew she was too angry to drive and she'd had quite a bit of champagne too, so she stormed off to the kid's room, retrieved Cassie, called a cab and went home. When she got home, she called Tina and made arrangements for her to go to the hotel and get her car. It was only about half an hour before Tina showed up at her doorstep to get her car keys. Tina left a male friend sitting in his car while she pried the whole story out of Lanie before leaving to pick up the car.

Tina's parting shot as she left was, "Who does he think he is anyway? Betting on you, who does he think you are, Secretariat?"

Chapter Five

As soon as he got to work the next day, Frank cornered Laura in her office. It was not a good day to bother her. She was utterly beleaguered and almost hidden completely by a very tall stack of reports and various computer printouts.

"Hey kid, I need your help." Frank leaned in her door; he couldn't help grinning at her expression.

For once, Laura didn't seem the least bit glad to see him. Her usual warm smile and sunny disposition were noticeably lacking.

"Frank, if it's not business, call me at home later, please," she said tiredly but firmly before she looked up with a wan smile. "With Bob and Kate both gone, I have two brand new temps here. And of course those temps need more supervision than I have time to give them, so I have all the work I can possibly handle. Now I know why two people from one office should never marry each other, the honeymoon is hell on the rest of the staff."

"I'm surprised Bob didn't have everything covered before he left," Frank said. "Kate didn't know they'd be gone, but he did."

"I think he tried to get everything done that he could," Laura said, "but there's some jerk at corporate who requested the financial reports from the last quarter a full week early. I tried to reason with him but he wouldn't even listen."

"Is there anything I can do to help?" he offered. "I have a lot of my own work to do today but you know I'll do anything I can to help you. Let me call the jerk and see if I can reason with him."

"Hey! In spite of reports to the contrary, you *can* take a hint!" She laughed at him and gave him the name of the jerk.

He left her office only to return a short time later. "The jerk wouldn't budge. I think he's jealous because he never had a honeymoon."

"Couldn't he get off for it?"

"No. He just couldn't find anyone stupid enough to marry him," Frank quipped. "Is there anything else I can do to help?"

"There sure is." She grinned as she handed him a large stack of papers. "You can start on the past due Receivables. Make sure they're all billed, and that the bills are sent out. If there are any current Receivables in that bunch, just file them. Get one of the temps to help you. Then, call any of these that are over thirty days late and politely demand payment. If they are over 90 days late, don't be quite so polite. Document all your calls, and mail letters restating any payment agreement you reach with any of their accounting managers or controllers. Then make me an aging report so that I can follow it all up. Got it?"

"Got it. But before I get to work, can you give me an idea on how to proceed with Lanie? Any idea at all?" He grinned. "The last time I saw Lanie at the wedding she told to me, and I quote: 'I don't want to see you, I don't want you to call me, just leave me alone' in those exact words."

"So?" Laura said without looking up from her paperwork. "Do not let her see you and do not call her, but definitely, and I mean definitely, do not leave her alone."

"So what should I do?" Frank tried to bring the conversation back to the main point. "What's my next step?"

"I don't know. Let me brainstorm out loud. You could write her, maybe send her flowers and gifts."

"Gifts?" Frank was surprised. "What kinds of gifts?"

"Nothing expensive or fancy. Just send her little gifts, trinkets and cute things, use your sense of humor more than your wallet." Laura paused, thinking before she continued, "Just don't send her anything crude or insulting."

"Would I do that?" Frank yelped.

"Sure you would, but don't. Do whatever you can think of to intrigue her and keep her a little off balance, and drive her just a little crazy." Laura thought for another minute. "Maybe what Lanie needs is a secret admirer."

"I see two problems: One, a secret admirer is too obvious, she'd guess it was me in a second. She's not stupid." Frank grimaced. "And two, it's corny, very corny, and I am a very suave and sophisticated kind of guy, macho too." He pointed at his chest and winked lecherously at her. "It's not my style and you know it, Babe."

"Yeah sure, Frank." Laura barely managed to avoid laughing out loud. "Suave and sophisticated, macho. Those are the very words I think of every time I see you."

"You should," Frank said with mock indignity.

Frank took his stack of papers and left in a huff when Laura finally started to laugh herself sick. He asked one of the temps to help him, found an empty cubicle, and got to work. Laura's suggestions were never far from his mind the whole day. He never knew that Laura got a phone call from Kate later that day, and he definitely never knew exactly how much of the conversation revolved around Lanie and him.

"A secret admirer, umm, clever idea, is he going to do it?" Kate asked, interested.

"I don't think so," Laura told her sounding disappointed. "He thinks it's too obvious and much too corny for a suave, sophisticated and macho kind of guy like him. His words, not mine."

"I wonder what Frank would do if Lanie had another secret admirer?" Kate queried.

"Another secret admirer?" Laura said, intrigued.

"Yes, another secret admirer. One who wasn't him?" Kate mused, then she giggled. "I've got to go, Laura, something's come up."

"I'll bet you dollars to a donut it's something on Bob." Laura laughed. "I've had a great honeymoon, too."

"You'd win the dollars." Kate hung up.

Just about three days after the wedding, Lanie found an envelope addressed to her on the front seat of her truck as she left for work. Opening it, she found a note that read:

You are now the proud owner of one brand new secret admirer, fully equipped and totally devoted; he comes with a lifetime guarantee for love.

Lanie smiled knowing it was from Frank, and knowing that she was still planning on making him pay for betting on her like, in Tina's not very flattering phrase, a prize racehorse. Secretariat indeed! He would pay and pay dearly! If Frank thought winning her was going to be that easy, boy, was he wrong!

The next day she found a second note. This time on her doorstep. This one was different, for one thing it was typed, it read:

Everyone bets once in a while but not everyone wins. Take a chance on your secret admirer and lay down a bet on love, to win.

There was an envelope with a ticket to Santa Anita Racetrack, a tout sheet and five $2.00 bills in it. The next day she found another note. This time it was just a note, handwritten, no gifts.

The fourth note, a day later, included flowers, red roses:

I know you work with plants all day, but sometimes flowers are just for play, and sometimes they mean something special. These mean love. Your secret admirer

Soon, it seemed like Lanie was getting notes and small gifts almost every time she turned around. One day, she found an unmarked cassette in the tape deck of her car. When she turned it on she heard Doris Day singing, *Once I Had A Secret Love*. Some of the notes were written by hand and some were typed. She noticed that not all of the handwritten notes had the same handwriting. A couple of them were in the form of limericks.

One of them read:

> *There once was a secret admirer*
> *Whose passion grew ever higher*
> *But the one that he loved*
> *Pushed, shouted and shoved*
> *Him away, 'stead of drawing him nigher.*

She never saw any of the notes or gifts as they were being delivered, but she thought they were all from Frank. At least, that's what she thought before she noticed the discrepancy in the handwriting.

Her favorite notes came with a small pearl in each envelope. The first one also included a length of sturdy string and a needle. It read:

String these up as soon as each one comes with a strong double knot in between and when we're more than secret chums, you'll have something to make others green.

A few days later it was followed by a note that came with a bottle of expensive cologne:

There's a scent of romance in the air, can you smell it? Your secret admirer.

When she went to take out her garbage, she found a note on the trash can:

A secret admirer is a terrible thing to waste.

In her rose bushes she found:

Let my secret admiration for you blossom into full bloom.

On her front door she found a cartoon of a sad-faced clown that simply read:

A secret admirer needs love, too.

But the gifts continued. A box filled with lacy underwear

came with a note that read:

I'm panting for your love. Your secret admirer.

With a scratcher lottery ticket:

I've got an itch to scratch. Your secret admirer.

Another limerick turned up:

> *There once was a secret admirer*
> *Who loved one with fire and with ire*
> *She was a real redhead*
> *Who he should have bedded*
> *But her temper was really most dire*

Another note that came with a decorated gift box read:

I'd love to put rings on your fingers and bells on your toes, but will you settle for bracelets and earrings instead? Your secret admirer.

Soon, she had four brand new bracelets, three sets of earrings, a stuffed Teddy bear, six brands of cologne, and even a dozen pairs of lacy underwear in various pastel shades, plus ruby red, emerald green and royal blue, not to mention basic black.

The weird thing was, Frank never called her and he never came over. She sat by her phone night after night but never admitted, even to herself, that she was waiting for him to call. Finally, she decided to call him. When she did, the infuriating rat wasn't home or he wasn't answering. She left a message on his machine. He never called back. The next day she called his office and asked for Laura.

"Frank's been on a business trip, Lanie. He's in Texas," Laura told her. "He's been gone for almost two weeks now."

"Then who's been sending me all those corny secret admirer notes and gifts?" Lanie asked. "Did Frank ask you or Kate to send them while he was gone just to keep me off balance?"

"No, of course not," Laura told her, "and I can answer for Kate, too. Heck, she's so busy on her honeymoon I don't think

48

she'd have time to write a secret admirer note, let alone send it."

"Well, it's funny and sweet, and corny, and silly and it's driving me nuts--but if it's not Frank behind these notes, then who is it?" Lanie said, "That's kind of spooky."

After she hung up, Laura dialed Kate. "We have her intrigued and a little spooked, Kate. She knows Frank didn't send the notes, at least not all of them. I don't think she has a clue."

"Doesn't she suspect us?" Kate's voice sounded strange, breathless. "I would if I were her."

"Well, she did. She asked me straight out if Frank had asked us to deliver the notes for him while he was gone. I said no, but I didn't volunteer anything else," Laura replied. "And what's wrong with your voice?"

"Well, he didn't ask us to send the notes," Kate said smugly. "He doesn't even know about it. And nothing's wrong with my voice, it's just that Bob's here with me."

"Oh, I see. Honeymooners. Well, the gifts you added to go with the notes were a nice touch," Laura complimented Kate.

"What gifts?" Kate was puzzled. "I didn't send any gifts."

There was an ominous silence before Laura asked, "You haven't included any gifts? No lottery tickets, bracelets, lingerie?"

"No, not a thing, and you?" Kate asked.

"No, nothing." Laura paused. "And she's had a lot of gifts including items of jewelry, cologne, lacy lingerie, lottery tickets, roses, even loose pearls complete with needle and thread," Laura itemized. "It's got her almost scared, except that deep down she really thinks it's all from Frank."

"Oh, oh." Kate summed it up. "If it's not Frank, then who is it? Who's her secret admirer?"

That night Bob listened as Kate told him all about the secret admirer, admitting that she and Laura had sent some of the notes, the limericks, but not any of the gifts.

"Do you think Frank's sending them somehow?" Kate asked.

"Even from corporate headquarters?"

"Kate, he's out of state, and these things are being hand delivered all hours of the day and night. How could he be doing it?" Bob questioned reasonably. "The only ones he would trust to deliver gifts and notes are you and Laura, so it's not him."

"Are you and Jack up to something?" she asked him suspiciously. "I don't trust either one of you."

"I'm 'up to' continuing my honeymoon." He kissed her without really answering her question.

"Yes sir, O mighty husband and boss. Good idea." She pulled him to her and ended all conversation for the night, except for a few moans.

Jack and Bob conferred by phone the next day. Neither one knew just who was sending the gifts, although they had each sent some of the notes.

"Kate and Laura are freaking, trying to figure out if Frank's doing this or if someone else is after Lanie," Jack said.

"Both of them have sent some notes, too," Bob said. "Laura told me that some days Lanie gets two or three separate deliveries. She and Kate are aiming at every other day."

"And you and I are filling the days in between, and driving our wives crazy." Jack laughed.

"Yeah. Isn't it fun?" Bob sounded smug. "It's hard to get either one of them thrown off balance, and right now we've got them both reeling. Even Kate's worried that someone may really be stalking Lanie."

"But I wonder who's giving Lanie the gifts. I really hope it's not a creep. There's all kinds of weirdoes running around out there these days," Jack said before he went back to work.

Laura called Tina. "What do you know about the secret admirer's letters and gifts that Lanie's been getting lately?"

"When Frank first told me he was going to do it, I thought it was a great idea. While he was out of town I even sent a few notes every two or three days, but no gifts," Tina told her, not noticing that Cassie, sitting beside her, was grinning from ear to ear.

"Grandma," Cassie said excitedly into the phone later that night, "it's working. It's really working. They don't have a clue."

"Okay, Honey," her grandma told her, "here's what you do next--"

Meanwhile, Lanie sorted out the notes by the handwriting and different type styles, along with the differing content of the messages. She figured out that there had to be at least seven different secret admirers. As near as she could guess they were: Kate and Laura, Bob and Jack, Tina, Frank. She bet that one of them sent the pearls, and someone else, the one who sent all the small gifts.

She believed that Kate and Laura sent the Limericks. Bob and Jack had sent the notes on her trash can and in her rose bush, among others. Tina was behind the clown drawing on her front door. Frank was responsible for the first note and all of the notes that came with the pearls.

The only one she couldn't guess the identity of was the person behind the other gifts. That was mystifying and almost spooky.

That last one had her perplexed. Who was it? The whole thing was like a soap opera and Lanie decided she could hardly wait for the next exciting installment.

The pearls had been turned into a beautiful necklace. There was a small diamond band about a quarter of the way around the necklace, followed by an emerald that hung down from the middle of the necklace and another diamond band about a quarter of the way back to the clasp at the back of her neck. It really was an exquisite piece of jewelry.

If Frank had handed her an expensive piece of jewelry like that, she would have felt obligated to refuse to accept it. She wasn't sure what to do about it however since he had given it to her pearl by pearl. Was each pearl a separate gift? She sighed realizing that she was fooling herself, she couldn't accept the necklace even if he did send it one piece at a time.

She reached out to pick up the phone and realized that she had trapped herself. She couldn't give the necklace back without calling him. She groaned remembering the look on his face when he had said that she would be the one to call him first. Oh hell, she thought, I can't call him without making him think he's right. She decided to wait a few days to think it over.

The very next morning a solution presented itself. The latest gift from her secret admirer included a brochure and a ticket to a weekend trip on a mystery train for the coming weekend, along with a note that simply read:

It's no mystery why I care so much. Please? Your secret admirer.

Intrigued and infuriated she decided to go, if for no other reason than to tell the big jerk off. At least that's what she told herself.

Frank didn't know when he decided to follow Laura's advice to become Lanie's secret admirer that he wouldn't be the only one. He only knew that he had to do something original. He found an absolutely stunning pearl necklace and then cut it up, sending the pearls out one by one. Small gifts that would add up to something special.

Like Lanie, he realized that there were other secret admirers and he figured out who most of the others were. All except one. All except the one who sent small gifts, and that made him mad as hell. Sending Lanie gifts, especially jewelry and lingerie, was his territory, his exclusive territory. The word jealous never entered his mind.

He was going crazy waiting for Lanie to call him and say she couldn't accept the necklace like good, decent women always do, so that he could then fight it out with her. What gave her the nerve to accept intimate gifts from strangers anyway?

Then came the day when he found a note on the front seat of

his car. It read:

It's my turn. Please? Your secret admirer.

Attached was a ticket to a mystery train.

Chapter Six

Lanie was both excited and apprehensive about the upcoming weekend aboard the mystery train. She wasn't really sure if she wanted to go but she couldn't bring herself to stay home. She wasn't even sure which clothes she wanted to take. Should she take plain, comfortable clothes or something fancier?

There was only one thing she was sure of, she didn't want to be teased or to face any speculation from either of her partners, especially Jack, about exactly why she was leaving early on a Friday night. She avoided that by working right up until five o'clock. That's why she only had about an hour after leaving work to shower, change, and get to the train station. Tina was already at her house, waiting to take her to the station. Tina would stay in the house with Cassie for the weekend.

Lanie was extremely nervous about the weekend. There were so many questions whirling around inside her head, she was glad no one could see into her brain. She kept thinking of questions like: Was Frank the secret admirer behind this trip? If not, who was? What would she do if it were Frank? What would she do if it weren't Frank? No stupid, she told herself, it's Frank. It has to be Frank. Could Kate and Laura have set this up?

Then there were the other questions, things like: Wasn't she mad at Frank about something? If so, what was it? She seemed to have forgotten, exactly. Something about a bet. But then, like he had pointed out, what kind of man would bet his whole future just to win lunch every week for a year? Did she have to give him back all the gifts? Or just the necklace? What about the lingerie? She really should return the lingerie. Damn!

And why was she such a klutz every time she saw the man?

She never had accidents; she was usually as agile as a cat. Did Frank make her nervous? Why? And why was he such a klutz every time he saw her? Lanie would bet her last nickel that Frank didn't have a clumsy bone in his body.

There's probably a million reasons why she should skip the trip and avoid Frank, she told herself, but on the other hand, she couldn't really think of even one really good reason, and this trip sounded like it would be a lot of fun. It had been a long time since she had a fun weekend just for herself.

There was a brochure along with the ticket that specified casual clothes except for the formal Saturday night dinner, which was to be held at an old country inn in Monterey Bay. The brochure also gave hints and rules for solving the mysteries. Finally it explained that all meals were prepaid, but bar drinks were not.

Lanie already had everything all packed and waiting in her car, ready to go. She had picked out all her best shorts and slacks, including soft sweaters and several T-shirts. Her casual clothes were attractive, comfortable and practical but also nothing special. She wanted Frank to realize that she was there to relax and have some fun, not because she was interested in him. As far as she was concerned, she told herself, she could have as much fun if Frank weren't even there. Sure she could, she admitted ruefully, facing some of her feelings. Not!

Since she was running late for the train, she let Tina drive to the station. Tina had the spirit of a race car driver, fast, but always completely safe. Cassie rode in the backseat. They got to the station just in the nick of time.

Tina helped her unload the luggage which they then gave to a very young porter. She barely had time to give Tina and Cassie a hug before she had to board the train. Lanie was nervous and excited as she kissed and hugged them both.

"Have fun, Mommy," Cassie told her. "I hope you and Frank solve the mystery and win the prize."

"I will sweetie. Be good for Aunt Tina, and make sure she behaves herself."

Cassie giggled, "Aw Mommy."

"Just solve the mystery of your love life," Tina quipped, hugging her, "and leave the murder mysteries alone."

"If I even have a love life, it's a mystery to me," Lanie told Tina. "Take care of Cassie for me."

She started to get on the train but stopped herself as a thought came to her. "Hey!" she asked Cassie. "How do you know Frank will be on the train?"

"I must have heard someone mention it," Cassie said evasively, looking sideways at Tina.

"It wasn't me!" Tina protested.

Lanie decided to let the matter drop and got on the train.

Frank was also running late for the train. He was just as puzzled about who had sent a ticket to him as Lanie was about her own ticket. The difference was, he didn't care! This realization was something of a shock to him. Bet or no bet he really wanted to see Lanie, but he seriously doubted that she wanted to see him. Oh no! He thought with a touch of panic, could he be falling in love? Part of him wanted to run, and part of him wanted to send Kate and Laura a thank-you note. No, he thought, that's premature. He decided to wait a while before he did either one.

Once inside, the train looked almost like a movie set, like the train in *Murder On The Orient Express*. Lanie found her compartment on the train and listened as the porter showed her the tiny washroom and bed, and the connecting door to the room next to hers. The compartment looked old-fashioned, it had panels on the walls that looked like wood, and a small fold-down bed. It reminded her of an old James Bond movie; she wasn't sure which one but it had Sean Connery as Bond.

When the bed wasn't down, there was a sofa and a small table. On the back of the compartment door there were hooks for her to hang some clothes. There was a luggage stand in one corner for her suitcase. There was also a small sink and counter for her cosmetics, with a tiny mirror.

The smiling porter accepted his tip and walked away, tipping his hat he said, "Dinner will be served in the dining car at eight. We start serving cocktails as soon as we leave the station. We're on time today so that should be within the next five minutes."

She heard someone settling into the adjoining compartment and impulsively opened the connecting door between them. She thought she knew who was there but she just had to find out.

"I knew it would be you." She greeted Frank with a wry smile. "You have been sending all those gifts and notes all along, including the pearls and the train ticket, haven't you?"

"All I sent were a few loose pearls and some string, no big deal." Frank shrugged, all the while watching her speculatively out of the corner of his eye, waiting for the explosion he knew was sure to come. "I don't know anything about any other gifts."

"No big deal!" Lanie protested. "Frank! That necklace is easily worth a king's ransom."

"Well, if a king ever gets kidnapped, we'll know enough to come to you," he quipped.

"Stop that right now, you idiot, this isn't a joke." She quieted her tone and continued in a more pleasant manner, "You'll have to take it back, you know, I can't possibly keep something so extravagant."

"I knew you'd say that." Frank paused before continuing slowly, "Do me a favor, Lanie. Please. Keep the necklace for a year, just one year, wear it and enjoy it. At the end of a year, if you still want to give it back, I'll take it with no argument."

"You mean that by the end of the year, when your bet is over, if we're not married you'll take the necklace back?" she clarified.

"Well, if I win the bet, we'll be married and you won't want to give the necklace back," Frank pointed out with a trace of logic, "and if I haven't won, you may still decide you want to keep the necklace as a token of all the aggravation I will have caused you. I'm sure there will be more aggravation, no matter how hard I try to prevent it. Either way, keep it and enjoy it for the year, please?"

"Okay." Lanie grinned at him. "I was fighting my conscience to keep it anyway. I love it. But I really do have to give you back the lingerie. There's no way for me to accept such an intimate gift."

"Lanie, I didn't give you the lingerie," Frank protested. "Honestly."

"Sure you did," she said slowly and firmly. "Who else would have sent me such an assortment of panties?"

"I don't know who could have sent you the panties but I did not," he said sincerely. "I don't even like to think about how you got them, about who else is sending you gifts. Please believe me."

"Really?" Lanie was incredulous. "Frank, are you telling me the truth, was it really someone else?"

"I swear," he said solemnly. "The only gifts I gave you were the pearls and the string. The only notes I sent you came with the pearls, except for the first note."

She looked into his face and saw the truth written there but still wondered about the ticket. Aloud, she said, "Okay, I'll keep the lingerie. It's very nice, anyway."

"Are you ready to go for a cocktail?" Frank asked. "The train has left the station."

"I hadn't even realized we were moving. I'd like to go for drinks but first, we have to settle the gift issue," Lanie replied. "Are you serious in saying you didn't send anything but the pearls?"

At his nod, she continued, "Then who sent the train ticket?"

"I thought you had," Frank said slowly.

"Me?" Lanie was so surprised her voice squeaked.

"I must have been fooling myself," Frank admitted. "I'd promised not to call you or visit you, so I thought, hoped really, that you'd sent the ticket as a way to see me."

"No way, Jose." She shrugged. He looked so disappointed she added, "Sorry."

"Well, remember I said the next time we got together it would have to be your choice and you would have to get in touch with me," Frank pointed out. "I tried to respect that but it wasn't easy. I really wanted to see you. I was hoping that the ticket had been your way of letting me know you had changed your mind about seeing me."

"But I didn't," she protested.

"If you don't want to see me, do you want me to leave?" he asked with deceptive calm. "If that's what it takes to make you happy, I'll go."

"No, of course not. That's not what I meant. I just meant that I didn't send the ticket. I guess I can stand your company for a weekend, besides," Lanie gave him an impish smile as she took his arm, "if you leave, who's going to buy me a drink?"

He was doing handstands in his head as he followed her to the club car where they had cocktails and then sat at a table and talked until dinner.

Just as the salads were being served, another couple came over and asked if they could join them. "There aren't any empty tables available," the woman explained, "and you're the only couple here that's even close to our age."

"Sure, we'd love to have you." Frank introduced himself and Lanie. "Please, sit down."

The other couple was Marilee and Paul. They were here for their third anniversary. "We thought we'd do something special this year because by our fourth anniversary we hope to have a baby," Marilee said, grinning.

The foursome talked their way through a very good chicken dinner. After dinner, there was an announcement by the train's mystery host. He explained that there were several actors among the sixty or so passengers on the train. They had been hired to act out parts of the murders, but with his help the regular passengers would have to be the detectives to solve the crimes.

The passengers would work in teams of two and there would be awards for the couple that solved the murder or murders first, of course, with the correct solution. There were also small prizes for finding various clues.

For each murder they would have to identify the victim, name the killer, point out how the victim was killed, why, and list the clues that led them to that solution. In the event of a tie, the team with the most correct clues would win.

"Remember," he warned them, "there might very well be more than one murder and more than one murderer aboard the train. If you find a body, remember to look around carefully for clues without touching anything. Please leave the crime scene intact for the other guests, then scream bloody murder," he winked. "Or at least tell either the porter or me so the rest of the passengers can come along and investigate the crime. If you find a clue anyplace other than a crime scene, study it then bring it to me so it will be available for everyone. We'll review these clues after every meal. You wouldn't want to take unfair advantage, or would you?"

"Sure I would," whispered Frank. "It's my competitive nature."

"Not me, I want to beat you fair and square," Lanie answered, challenging him. "Not that it will be very hard, you're no match for me. I've read all the Sherlock Holmes stories!"

"But you still can't beat me since we're not competing against each other," Frank said. "We're going to be partners and solve the murders together. Come on Lanie, please."

Lanie looked around pretending to think it over before she finally relented, "Since everyone else seems to be paired up already, I guess I'm stuck with you. You can be the brawns and I'll be the brains. Deal?" She grinned as she held out her hand.

"Deal." Frank reached out and shook hands with her. "But I

want it to go on record; I do have some brains."

Lanie patted his arm gently and said, "Sure you do, dear, sure you do." She cooed. "I know you're more than just a pretty face and a great bod."

"You think I have a great bod?" Frank grinned from ear to ear. "That's the nicest thing you've ever said to me."

"Don't let it go to your head, it was probably only temporary insanity," she stated archly. "I'm sure I'll recover before too long."

They mingled with the other passengers for a while until Frank suggested they go back to their compartments and talk.

Lanie thought quickly and then agreed. She wasn't sure what she was feeling for Frank but remembered a kiss that made her want to jump his bones on a public street in broad daylight, and a tingle in the pit of her stomach every time their eyes met. He intrigued her. He frightened her. No, she admitted silently, her own feelings frightened her but they were certainly worth exploring. She also realized with a start that she had never been bored in his presence. She had been angry, irritated, baffled and indignant maybe but never, ever bored.

"So?" Frank said as they walked down the corridor. "Your compartment or mine?"

"Let's open the door and make it ours. At least until bedtime," Lanie suggested.

"We could leave the door open until morning if you want." Frank wiggled his eyebrows in an exaggerated suggestion. "Or share one."

"I don't think so," Lanie singsonged to him before adding seriously, "we still haven't managed to spend a whole evening together without having an accident or an argument, not even once. Let's just get to know each other, okay?"

Frank gave her an innocent almost boyish grin. "Okay, but you can't blame a guy for trying."

"Keep trying, it's good for my self-esteem," she grinned, "and

I'll keep saying no. It'll be good for your humility."

"I don't have any humility," Frank pointed out.

"Stick with me, Kid, and I'll see that you get some," Lanie offered with an evil grin.

They each went into their own respective compartments. Lanie knew the mystery game was officially underway the moment she opened her door. There was no room for any doubt. There was a dead body lying on her compartment floor!

"Frank! Get in here, I need you." She quickly opened the connecting door.

"You finally realized it," Frank teased, entering her compartment.

"Not that, idiot." She gestured at the body. "Look!"

Together, they looked over the crime scene carefully. The corpse was a beautiful woman in her thirties, beautiful and dressed in a slinky peignoir. There was no blood, no visible wounds or other signs of violence; neither Frank nor Lanie had seen her before.

The single letter "R" was written on the wall in lipstick, a shade too red to be Lanie's. On the nightstand there were two champagne goblets, one with lipstick on it. Both glasses had a small amount of what appeared to be champagne in the bottom.

"Who's R?" Lanie asked.

"Probably a red herring, a tribute to Sherlock Holmes from, I think it was, *A Study in Scarlet.*"

"No, you fool," Lanie dismissed the idea. "That was the word Rache. Inspector Lestrade thought it was a woman named Rachel, remember?"

"He was wrong, as I remember," Frank said.

"Lestrade was always wrong," Lanie agreed.

"What did the word mean in the book?" Frank asked.

Lanie thought for a minute then said, "Revenge. It was sort of a red herring in the book."

"Enough about Sherlock," Frank told her, "we'd better find

the porter and report this murder." He started towards the door.

"Wait! Let's make it really exciting." Lanie winked at Frank and then let out a bloodcurdling scream.

"There goes the neighborhood," Frank said with wry resignation in his voice as the other passengers came running.

The invasion lasted well over an hour while nearly sixty people poked and looked and speculated on everything in the room, Lanie and Frank included. One of the older gentlemen seemed especially surprised by the sight of the beautiful woman on the floor. Surprised and devastated.

While everyone was still trying to see all there was to see, Lanie had an idea. "Distract them," she whispered to Frank.

Frank walked to the doorway and peered into his compartment and said, "What in the heck is that?" as loud as he could.

Lanie took immediate advantage of the distraction and quickly sniffed both champagne goblets. Her hunch paid off; the goblet with lipstick on it smelled faintly of almonds. Was that cyanide or arsenic? She wondered vaguely.

Eventually the mystery host and the porter came in with a sheet and a stretcher and removed the body. The other passengers left, and Lanie and Frank were finally alone.

Pulling a bottle of champagne out of an ice bucket by his bed, Frank said, "I propose a toast."

"What to?" Lanie asked.

"To the first time we were together without spilling anything, especially all over you." He winked at her as he worked on the cork.

"Stand back while you--" Lanie almost got the whole warning out before the champagne fizzled all over her.

She was silent for a long moment, wet, cold and stunned. Then she saw the guilt and embarrassment on Frank's face and suddenly without warning, she laughed.

And laughed. And laughed. Her face turned purple, she was holding her sides, and there were tears streaming down her face while she continued laughing.

Frank began to think she was hysterical. He vaguely wondered if she would ever forgive him if he slapped her to snap her out of it. Luckily, she got herself under control before he came to a decision.

"Are you okay?" he asked with concern.

"My sides hurt," she told him, then asked, "Can you break a rib from laughing too hard?"

Finally Frank started to laugh too, a real laugh but not hysterical. "Lanie, if anyone could, my bet would be on you. I have to ask you though, why aren't you threatening me this time?"

"This outfit costs less than twenty dollars and can be used on my job, even if it's stained." She motioned to her denim shorts and tangerine tank top. "Remember, I dig in the dirt almost every day."

"Please never dress up around me again," Frank begged. "I liked this reaction better than the yelling."

"I don't want to sound rude," Lanie sipped her champagne, "but I'm tired and I'm going to bed, so lock the connecting door on your way out."

"No goodnight kiss?" he asked softly.

"No," Lanie smiled gently, "too dangerous."

Chapter Seven

Frank was both bewildered and bemused as he went into his suddenly too small and very much too lonely compartment. He was plagued by several questions. Could Lanie's last remark possibly mean what it sounded like? Was she actually afraid that one kiss might be too dangerous? Why? Could it be because a simple kiss could lead to something more? Was she fighting her attraction for him? Why? Would a kiss, even a simple goodnight kiss, force her to face her feelings for him? Is that what she meant by dangerous?

That parting remark could be significant. It could well be a sign that she was beginning to care for him. It could even be the best reason a woman had ever given for refusing to kiss him. Heck, Frank thought with a smug shrug, damn few women had ever refused to kiss him for any reason. He was still disappointed and frustrated, though.

"Lanie?" he called softly through the compartment door. "Have you ever heard what they say about making love on a train? The motion of the train is supposed to be highly erotic."

"When the time is right and we make love, big guy, we won't need the motion of a train to make the experience any more erotic. It's gonna be erotic enough. Believe me," she answered, laughing.

"Lanie?" Frank called softly. "You do realize that you just said *when* we make love? Not *if* we make love?"

Lanie groaned with exasperation, then caught herself and clarified, "Well, I meant, if it ever happens between us, not when. What are you anyway, a grammar teacher? Go to sleep."

"That's not what you said," Frank cajoled in a soft, dreamy

voice. "You said when, and that's what I'm going to dream about tonight. What will you be dreaming about?"

"Murder!" She laughed then continued sternly, "Forget it, Frank. It was a slip of the tongue," her voice dropped and the rest of her reply was soft and muffled but still firm, "or temporary insanity."

"A Freudian slip, I hope. I'm still feeling very hopeful." Frank whispered, "Good night, Lanie."

"Good night, Frank." Her voice was equally soft.

They both got ready for bed very quietly, each very conscious of the other and of the door that served as the only barrier between them.

That night neither of them slept very well in spite of the gentle motion of the train. Alone in their separate beds, both of them tossed and turned all night, each one very conscious of the other doing the same so very close by. Each tried to do their tossing and turning quietly, however, so that the other wouldn't hear them through the thin adjoining door.

The next morning Lanie quickly realized that her sister, Tina, had been into her suitcases. All the comfortable clothes she had packed were gone. Her shorts had all been replaced by newer, tighter and even shorter shorts, and all of her comfortable T-shirts had been replaced by tank tops and sweaters that seemed to have one feature in common, very low necklines.

Lanie must have been very tired or just plain blind last night not to notice the new, slinky black barely-there nightgown she'd found in the suitcase instead of her usual oversized t-shirt. Somehow she had worn the nightgown all night without even questioning its presence.

Lanie vowed revenge, somehow she'd sic Kate and Laura on Tina. Let them work their magic on her and mess around with her love life. Let Tina find out how it felt to be trapped and helpless, confused and frightened by the very intensity of her feelings, and unable to sleep. Then see how much she liked it!

Lanie vowed to call Laura someday soon, very soon.

"Nice outfit!" Frank said, as he eyed her appreciatively when they met for breakfast and compared notes on the murder from the night before.

Lanie looked down at the low cut peach tank top with its revealing cleavage and her very short, tight white shorts. "I'm glad you like it. Tina picked it out for me," she said ruefully. "She seems to have replaced all the comfortable clothes I packed. Everything in my suitcases now is either too tight, too short, or very low-cut; in other words, they're all way too revealing."

"I'll thank her when we get back," Frank joked with a leer that was only halfway a pretense.

"Don't bother, so will I," Lanie said, thinking to herself, I'll thank her with my fist. "I'll be sure to express my heartfelt gratitude."

During breakfast, they sat with the older gentleman they'd noticed from the previous night's crime scene and his wife. His name turned out to be Charles Wells, and his wife's name was Ellen. Charles was in his mid-sixties, gray-haired, very distin-guished looking and dapper. Charles' looks reminded Lanie of the Monopoly man from the board game. His wife was extremely well groomed, fit and trim. Her silver hair was superbly styled. She had avoided that purple or blue hue that so many women get on their gray hair. She had the look of someone who simply could not get dirty or mussed, no matter how hard she tried.

That morning Charles seemed a little sad and distracted. His attention wandered away from the lively conversation several times, and his hands shook as he barely ate his breakfast and drank his coffee. His friendly demeanor was stiff; it seemed forced and a bit unnatural. His wife was acting very loving and supportive but there was an element of suppressed tension in her, too.

In spite of that they seemed like a very close, devoted couple. They told Frank and Lanie that they'd been together for over forty years, married to each other for over thirty-eight. Charles, it turned out, was a highly successful Wall Street stockbroker. After breakfast Charles and Ellen left the table.

Frank and Lanie began to work on solving the crime. Surprisingly, they made a good team. Their personal styles balanced and complimented each other. Frank, more clerically inclined, sat at the table and kept the notes. Lanie, who tended to be more creative, paced around the room and brainstormed.

"I know it was poison and that it was put into the champagne," she said aloud. "But we have several unanswered questions."

"Let's list them," Frank said, also thinking aloud. "We have her name and description, but who was she really? What did she do for a living? Why was she on the train? Who did she know on the train?"

"Also, why was she in my compartment of all places? It appeared that she was using my compartment for a tryst, but with whom? Did the champagne indicate a friendly rendezvous, or was it actually there to calm her nerves and ease any hidden hostility between her and the person she was meeting?" Lanie added, pacing, "It might have been a man, well, probably, there was no lipstick on the second glass, besides why would she meet secretly with a woman? Who wrote the letter on the wall? Why? What did it mean? Was it just a red herring? Also, she knew Charles, but how well? He cared for her. Did you notice his reaction this morning at breakfast?"

"There was definitely something there," Frank agreed, adding, "and his wife knew about it, whatever it was."

Finally Lanie couldn't think any more. She needed a moment to herself. She turned Frank around and literally booted him out the door, kicking him gently on the butt.

"Go away for a while, I want to freshen up and change. I may even grab a short nap," she ordered.

Frank left reluctantly.

As he went through the door, Lanie called after him. "Nice butt!"

"Glad you like it." He turned and grinned. "It's part of the original equipment. I got it from my mom."

"I'll thank her when we get back." She shut the door. "She did pretty well by you, overall." The admission floated softly through the closed door.

"Lanie?" Frank said softly through the adjoining door. "I have many other sterling qualities from my mom. I even got a few from my dad. Would you like to know more about those qualities?"

"Don't tell me. Let me discover them on my own." Lanie chuckled. "It will keep the mystery alive."

"I'm a mystery?" Frank asked, surprised.

"Maybe enigma is a better word," Lanie replied softly. "Now, leave me alone."

"I'm an enigma," Frank whispered as he sat in his compartment smiling to himself.

At lunch, over a hearty meal of hot tomato soup and cold roast beef sandwiches, they discussed the murder with the other couple seated at their table. That couple, an electronics engineer and a schoolteacher, had been married for fifteen years. They had barely noticed the murders; instead they acted more like a honeymoon couple. They were so wrapped up in each other that it was hard to hold a conversation with them.

"I hope we're like that when we've been married fifteen years." Frank grinned.

"First, you have to convince me to marry you," Lanie challenged, "and that's not going to be easy, Big Fella."

After lunch, Frank and Lanie mingled and spoke with various guests. Most of the guests were couples between thirty and fifty. As a group, they tended to be bright and fairly well off. Frank and Lanie quickly spotted one or two actors among the guests. The actors were the only ones who knew anything about the victim.

The actors would circulate and gossip about the victim and various guests. From the gossip, Lanie and Frank learned that the victim was a famous socialite named Vera Stanhope. She had a scandalous past, including several affairs with movie stars and politicians. She was currently having an affair with a senator who was mentioned as a possible presidential candidate for the election almost four years away.

Not long after lunch, while Frank and Lanie were still talking with the other passengers, they heard a woman scream. Turning their heads, they saw a tall slender figure running down the narrow passageway away from the sound of the scream. Jumping up, they both followed the fleeing person at a dead run, only to lose their quarry. How they did that, in a narrow, straight, corridor was a mystery, even to them.

They gave up on the suspect and turned their attention back to the source of the scream. They fought their way through the crowd of passengers and found another dead body at the core of the mob. This time they were shocked. The victim was their breakfast companion, the older gentleman, Charles Wells. He had a gun in his lifeless hand and a bullet wound on his temple. Frank looked long and hard at the suicide note without saying anything.

Lanie seemed more interested in the man's wound. She also noticed the victim's wife Ellen sobbing over the body. Then she noticed Frank's preoccupation with the note.

Back at the compartment Lanie demanded, "All right, I saw how interested you were in the note, give. What is it?"

"The note was written by a right-handed person, I think a woman," Frank said importantly, "but the dead man was holding the gun in his left hand."

"Forged suicide note. That means it was a murder, right?" Lanie sounded impressed.

"Right." Frank was self-satisfied.

"Idiot!" She socked Frank in the arm. "We already knew it was a murder. It's a murder mystery, remember? Besides the wound was definitely not self-inflicted, there were no powder burns."

"But it's a clue," Frank pointed out, "just like your scent of almonds in the champagne glass."

"You're right." Lanie grinned unrepentantly. "Poor baby, did I hurt your arm?"

"Well, you could kiss me and make it better." Frank looked pitiful but there was a teasing glint in his eyes.

"Sure. No problem." Lanie leaned towards Frank and kissed the spot where she'd socked his arm. "Better?"

"Not really," Frank teased. "Maybe it would help if you kissed me on the mouth?"

"Why would a kiss on the mouth make your arm feel better?" Lanie asked warily.

"A kiss on the mouth, the right kiss, would make everything feel better," Frank teased again. "For both of us."

"Sounds like the right kiss would be magic," she murmured, moving closer to him.

"The right kiss is always magic," he said in a seductive tone.

"Sorry, Frank. Magic is something far too powerful for me to mess with." Lanie laughed and backed to the door of the compartment. Turning, she headed for the club car to get a cold drink.

During the afternoon a couple of clues were found by one passenger or another. A letter to Vera was found but its meaning wasn't very clear. It read:

Thanks for the rabbit. I'll skin him and put him in the pot. You just keep on adding the greens.

Your Pal

Another clue that was found by a passenger was a picture of Vera and Charles dancing. The picture, a Polaroid, was taken recently judging by the appearance of the couple, their ages and the style of their clothes. Besides, Frank pointed out with a grin, there was a date on the back of the picture, making it about four months old.

The pair was both formally dressed in the picture; Charles was in a tuxedo and Vera in a red flowing evening gown. They were obviously dancing to a slow dance and they were holding each other in an especially intimate looking embrace.

Around three in the afternoon, the train pulled into a station and the passengers were quickly unloaded and shuttled to a lovely old beachside inn. All the guests were efficiently checked in and shown to their rooms. By mutual agreement Frank and Lanie, who once again had connecting rooms, quickly unpacked, changed, and met in the lobby for a walk on the beach. They almost laughed aloud as they realized that their shorts matched, both the same exact shade of khaki. Along with the shorts Frank had on a blue polo shirt and Lanie a bright green tank top.

The afternoon was warm, but not hot enough for a swim. Frank had a large gray blanket and a thermos of something that he'd gotten from the hotel staff. He spread the blanket on the sand, set down the thermos and took Lanie's hand. They shed their shoes, walked along the beach listening to the squalling seagulls, and waded about knee deep into the cold water.

Lanie's small hand felt snug and secure in Frank's larger one and even though she wasn't ready to admit it to him, she relished the contact. Finally they turned and walked back to drop onto the blanket. They sat side by side and sipped orange juice from the cooler Frank had brought. Finally they laid down beside each other. Each one lay on their side and faced the other as they talked about the crimes comparing thoughts about the victims and the clues, keeping the conversation light and impersonal.

"It seems like Vera was involved with a blackmail scheme," Lanie said. "That's what the note must mean. She must have set up the victim and brought the greens."

"The greens?" Frank asked.

"The money," Lanie explained, "but who did she bring the greens to? She must have had a partner. And who was her victim?"

"Probably Charles," Frank said.

"It could be. I looked at his driver's license, his middle name is Randall." Lanie thought for a moment.

"So what does that tell us about who killed Vera and why?" Frank asked as he summed up the clues.

"Not a thing, really, just that she must have had a partner and other victims, therefore she had enemies. We already knew that, people who have no enemies seldom get murdered. Not like that." Lanie shrugged. "It gives us an area to investigate. We also need to find out for sure if her murder ties in with Charles' murder."

"It must," Frank speculated. "They knew each other as evidenced by the picture. What we need to know is: Was that dance an isolated incident or were they having an affair? Was that what was behind the blackmail."

"I'm voting for an affair as the basis for the blackmail," Lanie stated positively. "It's almost too obvious."

Frank grinned. "Which means there will be a twist attached."

Soon they fell into another discussion. As they sat side by side on the beach towel, Frank asked the question he'd been avoiding for a long time. "Lanie, I get the feeling that you're fighting your feelings for me, that you're holding something back. What's wrong? Is it something I've done?"

"No Frank." Without looking at him she took a deep sigh and thought for a moment. "You're right. I am holding back, fighting my attraction to you. It's nothing personal, nothing against you. I was hurt very badly once, long ago, and I don't want to risk that kind of pain again."

"Could you tell me about it? If not now, when you're ready," he asked gently.

"I will, soon," she promised, "but not yet."

"Lanie, you know I don't ever want to hurt you, don't you?" Frank looked into her eyes.

"I know, and I don't want to hurt you either," she smiled sadly, "but it's still frightening."

"And exciting?" he urged.

"And exciting," she agreed, noticing his sudden grin.

Before too long they went in and dressed for dinner. This was the one meal on the trip where formal wear was encouraged.

Lanie put on her make-up and combed her hair. Then she went to open her garment bag and soon discovered that true to form, Tina had replaced the evening dress she planned to wear with one that was much more revealing. It was also stunning. She started to put on the dress when there was a knock on her door.

"Lanie?" It was Frank.

She spread the gown on the bed, threw on a robe and opened the door. She noticed that he had a garment bag in his hands. "Hi Frank, what's that?"

"I *hope* it's a pleasant surprise and not a mistake. I thought maybe you'd want to wear it." He seemed apprehensive as he handed her the garment bag and left rather abruptly.

Intrigued, Lanie opened the garment bag and was stunned to see her white dress. It was the same one she'd worn when she met Frank, the same one that was irretrievably damaged by a combination of tomato juice and mud. It was in perfect condition. The only difference in this dress was the label; this was a handmade copy.

She was really touched by his consideration. She sat on the bed and stared at the copy for a long time. Finally she slid the dress on and stood there looking at herself in the mirror, tears welling in her eyes. It was perfect.

Then without really knowing or understanding why she did it, she took the dress off and hung it up again before putting on the sexy and more formal gown Tina had packed for her.

It was a moonlight blue sheath, made of the softest velvet, with thin spaghetti straps that crossed in the back. The straps were made of rhinestones. The plunging neckline and dropped back were also lined with the rhinestones. There was a slit in the dress from the floor length hem halfway up the thigh. Looking in the mirror, she was stunned. That couldn't be her! She was a tomboy who dug in the mud for a living. She was not really that woman in the mirror, that woman looked extremely glamorous and very sexy. She took a deep breath and went down to dinner.

As soon she entered the hotel's small dining room she saw Frank sitting at a table across the room looking very handsome in a dark suit. For once, her perspective when she looked at him wasn't tinged by anger or mistrust. Her reaction to him was the same, however. The familiar jolt in the pit of her stomach. Goodness, he's gorgeous, she thought. She took a deep breath before crossing the room to meet him.

Chapter Eight

Frank was sitting with some of the other mystery train guests when he looked up from his chair and felt dazzled as he spotted Lanie entering the ballroom. He smiled with genuine pleasure at Lanie just as she started to walk across the room. Stunned and entranced, he stood up and moved towards her, forgetting the other guests he had been speaking to at the banquet table.

She's terrific, he thought even as a part of him wondered vaguely why she wasn't wearing the dress he'd had made especially for her. He was a little bit disappointed but maybe she had a reason. Shrugging it off, he walked towards her almost in a daze. There was something to be said about the gown she was wearing, he realized. What little there was of it looked spectacular on her. How was it that a classy woman could wear a revealing, sexy dress and still look every inch a lady?

They met in the center of the room on the small dance floor just as the music started playing. It was recorded music, drifting in through hidden speakers. Without a word Frank and Lanie started to dance, moving slowly to the romantic music, holding each other closer than formal dancing allowed.

"You look stunning but I thought you'd wear the white dress," Frank asked her quietly. "Was it a mistake? Was I wrong to have it made for you?"

"No," she whispered, kissing him quickly, just a fleeting butterfly touch against his mouth that stunned them both. "It was definitely not a mistake. Having that dress made was the most beautiful thing anyone's ever done for me. I'm just saving the dress for another occasion. I'm not sure what, but I want to save it. It was an instinctive reaction. Trust me, Frank, please trust me?"

"Lanie? I don't want to claim all the credit," Frank admitted, "someone gave me the idea about the dress. I just don't want you to feel like I let you down or deceived you if you ever found out that when I had it made I was acting on somebody else's suggestion."

"But you were the one who had it made. That's what's important." She kissed him again. "Let me guess, was it Kate or Laura. Kate?"

"Good guess." He grinned at her.

He hugged her tightly for an instant before he whispered in her ear, "Do you like this song?"

"It's beautiful, a lovely old standard," she whispered back. "Who wouldn't like it?"

"Listen to the lyrics," he told her softly. "They say what I feel better than I ever could."

She thought for a minute, then stiffened slightly in his arms and her eyes opened wide as she realized what he meant. The song was: When I Fall In Love, and Nat King Cole was singing. She shivered at the phrase *"and the moment that I feel that, you feel that way too, is when I fall in love with you."* After a moment she sighed and relaxed in his arms again.

"They're beautiful lyrics," she whispered. "Very meaningful and touching."

"Not just sloppy and sentimental?" Frank questioned softly.

"Maybe so, but maybe I'm feeling pretty sentimental right now," Lanie told him, rubbing her cheek softly against his suit in an almost unconscious movement.

Although they had danced through the whole song, it seemed as though they had barely started when the music ended. They stood in place on the dance floor and waited for a moment.

Another song started and they began to dance again. They were still moving slowly almost dreamily, even though this song had a faster rhythm. After a while Lanie started to laugh softly.

"This song seems like an answer to the last one," Lanie explained. The song was: *What Do You Get When You Fall In Love?*

Softly she sang along with Dionne Warwick at the phrase, "*a guy with a pin to burst your bubble, that's what you get for all your trouble, I'll never fall in love again.*"

Frank groaned, leaning his forehead against hers. "I hope that's not your final answer." He laughed.

Lanie only laughed softly and sang the end of the song, "*and so for at least until tomorrow, I'll never fall in love again.*"

She shot him an impish grin before she said to Frank, "How could it be? The song just came on; I didn't have anything to do with the playlist."

Before he could reply the staff began to serve dinner. By mutual consent they made their way to their banquet table. The meal was truly wonderful.

They had crisp Caesar salads, succulent prime rib, baked potatoes with unlimited butter and sour cream, mixed vegetables steamed with a slight glaze, and fresh, hot sourdough bread. The dessert was a sinful choice between triple chocolate mousse pie and several kinds of cheesecake. Both Frank and Lanie went for the chocolate mousse pie.

After dinner they danced again. As the slow, romantic music worked its magic on them, they danced closer and closer together as though they were drawn by magnets.

"This is wonderful," Lanie murmured, relishing the feel of his hard body next to hers. She was more than conscious of a particular hardness pressing against her, telling her without words that Frank was moved, too. Even that hardness seemed right; instead of feeling lustful, it made her feel special and cared for.

"Is there going to be any murder mystery stuff tonight?" Frank whispered in her ear, nibbling softly and sending shivers up her spine. "Or are we on our own?"

"There's still some mystery stuff. I already asked the host," she whispered back. "He told me that only the Saturday night cocktail hour and dinner was time out, not the whole evening. In fact, there's a short meeting after dinner to go over the facts we've gathered so far and make sure that everyone has seen all the evidence."

"Damn!" He whispered urgently, "My mind is not set on solving any murders this evening."

"Oh? What is your mind set on doing?" she asked, grinning at him. "Anything in particular?"

For an answer, he rubbed himself up against her in a discreet but unmistakable invitation.

She flashed a wide-eyed look up at him. "Sir, I'm no expert on anatomy but I'm reasonably sure that's not your mind."

"It is, however, a prime indicator of the direction my mind is taking." Frank grinned.

"Just how prime it is, that's open for discussion. Maybe we can discuss it later," Lanie teased. "If the subject comes up again."

"I'll look forward to it," Frank assured her.

Just then, the mystery host appeared and the meeting was underway. He listed the clues without giving any interpretations to them. Thus far they were: For Vera Stanhope: The clues were the scandal sheet clipping, the picture of her with Charles Wells, the scrawled letter "R" on the wall, and a letter from Vera to someone named Randy stating that the affair was over and now he was going to have to pay to keep from going to jail. Something about stock manipulation, according to the letter.

"What letter?" Frank interrupted. "We've never heard of any letter. Aren't we supposed to see all the evidence?"

"Almost no one has seen it yet. It was just turned in by the team that found it," the host said. "I'll pass it around."

As the letter was circulated, the host continued the discussion with the murder of Charles Wells. The clues to his murder included: A forged suicide note and a gunshot wound to his head, with no apparent powder burns. That was all they had so far so the meeting adjourned. The dancing continued long into the night.

Frank and Lanie danced for a long time, savoring each other's company. It seemed like the time passed too quickly. They were shocked when the music finally stopped and the cleaning crew began to straighten up the dining room.

While it was still quiet, Frank and Lanie went outside for a while to soak in the evening air from the terrace. They stopped to lean against the gleaming white, wooden rail and drink in the aroma of a garden that had been planted especially to be as fragrant at night as it was beautiful during the day. The fragrances mingled with the scent of ocean breezes on the night air. It was a heady and romantic mixture.

Just as Frank took Lanie into his arms, one of the other mystery train guests bumped into her. It was Ellen, the newly widowed and sweet looking older lady. She was sobbing.

"Ma'am? Ellen?" Lanie said gently, steadying the older woman. "Are you okay?"

"Oh my dear, you're just too kind. I'm just not myself, after all my husband is--" The older woman sobbed and broke away, running off with surprising agility. There was a strange smell following in her wake.

Watching her leave it was hard for Lanie to believe only that morning, when they had eaten breakfast together, Ellen had been half of a couple. A couple who had spent almost every second together on the train. They seemed to be devoted to each other. They had been particularly supportive of each other at the first crime scene, and they had been a fixture at every social hour and meal until Charles was murdered.

"It's hard to believe that she's a widow now, just this morning she and Charles seemed so close, so loving." Lanie sighed sadly. "But I could see that there were undercurrents between them."

"There was something, very vague," Frank agreed. "A tension."

"Now she's alone after being married for so many years," Lanie said somberly. "That's so sad."

"That's no old woman, remember she's a part of the mystery," Frank reminded her as the woman ran off. "And she runs like a young woman. Her age is make-up and acting ability."

When Lanie looked at him with a question in her eyes, he shrugged. "Before I met you, I watched young women every chance I got, especially from behind."

"That must have been extremely hard for you to do." At his questioning look she explained, "I'll bet not too many women run away from you." Lanie laughed.

"Not until I met you." He hugged her, then he held her gaze as he continued, "All you seem to do is run away from me. I don't know what to do about it."

"Let's follow her," Lanie said, breaking the intense mood.

They followed the woman until they saw her stop and hide something under a rosebush. Then she disappeared into the garden. After she left, they dug around under the rosebush and found a small bundle. Frank pulled it out. Wrapped in a soft cloth, they found a used syringe and a woman's wallet. Lanie sniffed at the syringe. The syringe didn't have the scent of almonds. The wallet had a folded up newspaper clipping in it. It was a brief story about an investigation of insider trading by the SEC. No names were mentioned in the article. The wallet had a driver's license in it with the name of Caroline LaRue.

They examined these things closely before they took them to the mystery host. They wandered among the guests for a short time before going back to Frank's room. When they got there they ordered coffee from room service. They made themselves comfortable reclining on Frank's bed and discussed the case. Frank began listing all the clues they'd seen and everything they'd found on a tablet, along with a chronology of events.

"So who's Caroline LaRue?" Lanie puzzled.

"Beats me," Frank told her.

They needed to figure out who committed each murder, how, and why, along with listing their clues and reasoning. So far they had no idea of who the murderers were, or why the crimes were committed.

Eventually their discussion wound down and they realized that they were sprawled out on Frank's bed. Their eyes met and the air in the room seemed to sizzle. Lanie's breath caught in her throat when, without saying a word, Frank swept the notes aside and placed the coffee cups carefully on the bedside table. Just as Frank leaned slowly towards Lanie they heard a scream!

"Damn!" Frank muttered as they started for the sound of the scream. "Who said this would be a romantic trip?"

"Not me. I was surprised by the whole idea." Lanie quipped, "It must have been our mutual secret admirer."

"Secret matchmaker, you mean." Frank stopped as they came to the scene of the crime.

Frank and Lanie found a large group gathered in one of the hotel rooms. A rather heavy, middle-aged woman was dead with no apparent signs of injury. She was dressed in a flowing nightgown trimmed with feathers. She still had her make-up on, very heavy make-up.

The group did find, however, a syringe beside her body and one of those meters a diabetic uses to test blood sugar levels, along with several test strips. She also had a large amount of cash in her possession; they could see it flowing out of her purse. The whole group searched the room for other clues but nobody found anything. This time they found no clue as to the identity of the victim at the crime scene but Frank and Lanie already knew the reason for that. Her wallet and driver's license had previously been found, and the photo matched--she was Caroline LaRue!

As they went back to their rooms Lanie stopped at her door. "Frank, I don't think we should--, well, I think we were about to get carried away back there before the scream and--" She shrugged. "Heck! I'm saying this badly. I want you, but I'm just not ready to sleep with you yet. I hope you understand."

"Is this the part where I say that I understand?" Frank leaned over and kissed her on the forehead. "That I don't want you unless you're sure the time is right? I understand. I don't like it much, but I do understand."

The next morning Lanie awoke from a very restless sleep with the solution to all the murders firmly fixed in her mind. She called Frank, who was still asleep, and told him to put on a robe and come to her room. Then she pulled on her own robe and got into action before Frank ever had a chance to join her.

Quickly she got a sheet of paper then sat at the small table in her room and began to write all her ideas, spelling them out in a neat orderly fashion, ready to turn in as their guess for the solution. Frank got to the room just in time to stand there and watch as she worked on the paper, making suggestions from time to time. She wrote:

VICTIM 1
NAME: Vera Stanhope
HOW KILLED: Cyanide in her champagne
KILLED BY: Charles R. Wells, AKA: Randy
REASON: Vera was being blackmailed for certain indiscretions in her very scandalous past because she was engaged to marry a prominent senator who was thinking of running for president. Among her indiscretions was an affair with Mr. Wells, a Wall Street financier who gave her lots of trinkets, which he paid for with insider trading. Vera made a deal with her blackmailer: in exchange for an end to her blackmail, she had told the blackmailer about some of Mr. Wells' illegal activities such as insider trading and pilferage of some old folk's retirement accounts.
CLUES: The two champagne glasses, the scandal sheet clipping about her wild affairs, the smell of almonds on her champagne glass, the letter R on the wall, a letter to Randy

telling him that the affair is over and now he's going to be the one to pay for it. The picture of Vera slow dancing with Mr. Wells.

VICTIM 2

NAME: Charles R. Wells

HOW KILLED: Gunshot to the head

KILLED BY: Mrs. Charles R. Wells, Ellen

REASON: She had just found out about his affair with Vera Stanhope and was furious not only about his affair with a younger woman, but also that he was stupid enough to finance the affair by committing criminal acts that threatened her future. Their nest egg would be spent on legal fees and her good name in society would be ruined. Also her dream of spending the rest of her life in relative comfort with a loving husband was forever shattered.

CLUES: The forged suicide note was in her handwriting, according to the analysis, and she was the only one who could get close enough to do it. She found the body simply because she did the killing. Her suspicious acts on the night of the party, including hiding the bundle of evidence. The tall figure running down the hall was a red herring; he was going to get the porter to report the crime.

VICTIM 3

NAME: Caroline LaRue

HOW KILLED: Insulin Shock

KILLED BY: Vera Stanhope

REASON: She was the blackmailer. She had made a deal with Vera to discontinue the blackmail if Vera told her everything she knew about Randy Wells' illegal activities, but she reneged on it. She was going to continue to blackmail both of them.

CLUES: A note to Vera saying, in a roundabout way: Thanks for giving me another person to blackmail but the

payments must continue. A second, almost invisible, hole in the vial of insulin. Large amounts of cash. Traces of glucose in the insulin vial. The syringe found by Lanie and Frank.

"So?" Lanie looked at Frank expectantly. "What do you think?"

"How could Vera kill Caroline? She was already dead." Frank was puzzled.

"That insulin could have been poisoned at any time," Lanie pointed out. "She knew that sooner or later Caroline would have to use it. It's a safe poison, too. There's no chance of someone else taking it by mistake."

"What do you mean?" Frank needed clarification.

"Well, if you poison something like a bottle of wine, you have to be very careful that an innocent bystander doesn't get the poison instead of your intended victim. Who wants to go to death row for the wrong victim?"

"That would be a bummer." Frank nodded agreeably.

"But with a prescription medicine, you wouldn't have that worry." Lanie continued, "You could put the poison in and just stand back and wait."

"It's frightening how your mind works." Frank shivered.

"You'd better believe it, Bub," she told him with an evil laugh.

"I still don't know if I agree that Vera killed Caroline but I haven't got any better suspect. Let's go turn it in," Frank returned to the subject. He planted a quick kiss on Lanie's mouth. "Partner."

They gave the solution to the mystery host who wrote the time on it and looked it over without a word as to its contents. He did have one thing to say, however.

"You do know that if anything else happens, you may have to revise this?" he questioned them.

Sure enough, something else happened. Ellen Wells was found dead of a gunshot wound to the head. Lanie grabbed her tablet and wrote simply:

Ellen Wells: faced with arrest in the death of her husband, committed suicide.

She handed the paper back to the host. Then she and Frank went into the dining room and ate breakfast at the inn. It was another great meal with heavenly omelets filled with ham and cheese, bacon, large glasses of orange juice, and homemade blueberry muffins. They even had time for another long stroll on the beach before it was time for them to get back on the train.

Chapter Nine

The Mystery Train's return trip was much faster than the trip to the inn had been for several reasons. For one thing, they traveled a shorter route, and for another, the train itself traveled at a slightly faster speed. There was a final meeting for the passengers in the club car shortly before lunch, the last meal to be served aboard the train.

"Ladies and gentleman, I've reached my decision on the winner of the grand prize." The mystery host stood at the center of the room and made his announcement.

Lanie's keen sense of competition took over. She reached over and took hold of Frank's hand, squeezing it gently. Frank was surprised at her action but returned the gentle squeeze. Together, still holding hands, they waited to hear the announcement.

The host prolonged the suspense by reading some of the wrong guesses first. Frank and Lanie listened but none of their solutions were read as being incorrect. With Lanie's fingers crossed and still holding hands, they waited while the host read the winning guess. The answer to Vera's murder matched theirs. The answer to Charles' murder matched theirs. Lanie and Frank tightened the hold on each other's hand! The solution to Caroline's murder was read. It matched theirs, too!

The mystery host told the group that two teams actually had all the correct answers, including Ellen's suicide, but only one team had listed the clues correctly. He said he would name the second place team first, without reading their solution. Then he would read the correct solution and the first place team. He named the second place team. It turned out to be an older couple from Oxnard traveling in celebration of the husband's retirement. They stood up, seeming a bit embarrassed, while everyone applauded them and the mystery host gave them each a Mystery Train plaque naming them Detective First Class, Second Place, and discounts on a future stay at the country inn where the guests had spent Saturday night.

By that time, Frank and Lanie knew they'd won but they continued to grasp each other's hands. The mystery host read their solutions, listed their clues, and then he read their names: Lanie McPherson and Frank Morgan. They'd won! They gave each other a quick hug, and an equally quick kiss, before they went up to claim their prizes. They each received wall plaques like the second place couple had and won a weekend stay for two at the country inn, but they received one more thing. There was a cash prize of $200.00 each. Lanie immediately handed her share of the winnings to Frank.

"On account," she said, "for the damage I did to your brand new car at Laura's party."

"No way, Lanie love." Frank handed her back her money along with his. "This goes to buy a new bike for your daughter, Cassie. She was telling me about wanting a bike when I met her at Kate and Bob's party, or their wedding, whatever the heck it was."

"I already got her a bike." Lanie smiled. "It was used but in very good condition and I had it repaired and repainted. She really loves it. A brand new one couldn't have made her any happier."

"I'm glad." Frank grinned at her. "I liked her when I met her, she seems very sweet."

"Like her mom?" Lanie asked mischievously.

"Don't push your luck," Frank teased. "Her mom is many things, and has many wonderful qualities, but sweet isn't one of them."

"Gee, thanks a lot," Lanie muttered, then laughed as Frank gave her a quick, searing kiss.

That quick peck when the winners were announced had been just enough to grab his interest. The second kiss added to it. He decided to act, moving to kiss her again. This time he intended to make it a real kiss, long and passionate, but the opportunity was lost as Lanie turned her attention to the couple who had finished in second place.

That couple and Lanie congratulated each other. Frank made the appropriate friendly noises, but he was impatient for the other couple to leave them alone. Finally the other couple left. Frank could barely contain a sigh of relief; he still wanted to give Lanie a real kiss, not just a congratulatory peck! Real kisses had been few and far between in this romance!

Just then the waiter came over and asked for their lunch orders. Frustrated, Frank put the kiss on hold until the waiter left. It seemed like it took the waiter forever. He poured coffee and ice water for both of them while they made their choices from a simple selection. They both decided quickly and ordered tossed salads, fried chicken, mashed potatoes and country-style biscuits. The waiter finally left and Frank took advantage of the peace and quiet to return his attention to Lanie.

He reached out and gently stroked one hand over the softness of her cheek, turning her to face him. He leaned across the table and kissed her gently but with real passion. The kiss lingered for just a moment on her lips before the familiar and unsettling jolt hit them both and her mouth opened with a soft moan granting him access.

"Let's spend the money together then, on the two of us having fun." Frank pulled back, remembering that they were in a public place. He suggested, "With four hundred dollars we could--"

"No way, Buster. Half of this is my money. I get to spend it however I want. I owe you the money to fix your car and that's what I want to do with it," Lanie insisted. "It's only a start to what I owe you."

"Okay, if you want to be stubborn about it. I'll take the money less the cost of the two dresses I ruined," Frank conceded.

"But you replaced the white dress," Lanie protested. "You can't pay me for a dress that you've already replaced."

"The emerald dress then, the one you wore to Kate's surprise wedding," Frank countered. "I haven't replaced that one."

"No way! That wasn't your fault, you are not paying for it." Lanie's chin was raised stubbornly. "One of the kids bumped into you, remember?"

Frank saw a spark of combat in her eyes, a flush on her cheeks, and noticed her breathing was rapid. He couldn't resist. Like a man who tries to pet a caged tiger, he reached out and verbally stroked her temper.

"I'll pay for the dress if I want to pay for the dress and there's not a damn thing you can do about it!" he said sternly. "I'm not letting you pay for the damage to my car. There's something you should know: part of the accident was my fault because I was the one who broke your mirror."

"You what?" Lanie was astonished.

"I bumped into a car at the party. I didn't know if I broke anything because I didn't see any damage. I really did look," Frank admitted.

"So you just ignored it?" Lanie was suspiciously quiet.

"I'm afraid so. I was pretty sure I broke your mirror but like I said, I couldn't find any damage. It was dark and the cars were all jumbled together. Let's face it neither one of us was really to blame, that parking was an accident waiting to happen," he said. "I'm not even sure if I broke a mirror or just bumped one fairly hard. I just don't want you to pay me for any damages."

"You never told me this before?" Lanie's voice rose as she continued, "I was trying to figure out how to pay for the damage and you never mentioned breaking my mirror? I'm still responsible for the damage to your car."

"And I'm still not letting your pay for it." Frank stated positively before adding, "Also, I'll buy you any gifts I want to, when I want to, and you'll accept them and like it!"

"You just can't go around buying me things and force me to accept them," Lanie raised her voice, "especially expensive things like the pearl necklace and expensive evening dresses."

"I can if I want to." Frank met her head on, leaning forward so that he was almost nose to nose with her across the small table. "Just try to stop me!"

"You're just trying to buy me. Jerk!" She fumed. "Like this trip. You're just irritated because you went to all this time and trouble to get the tickets for this trip and you didn't even get to go to bed with me."

"I told you before, I didn't buy the tickets." Frank lost his own temper now. "Believe it or not, whichever you choose. I will admit to wanting to go to bed with you. I want to make love to you and I think you want it too. If that's a crime, I'm guilty! Is that really such a terrible crime?"

Before she could answer the waiter returned and served their lunch. She waited politely for the harried man to leave their table before replying to Frank.

"It is terrible when you treat me like the prize in a box of Cracker Jacks instead of a woman." She exploded. The fight was on for real now. "I'm a real person, damn it! I have a right to be treated with some concern for my feelings, my reactions, my plans and my dreams."

"I do have concern for your dreams. I care for you. I don't want to treat you like a toy prize, I want to treat you like a real woman, a woman I treasure," Frank stormed at her. "Admit it! You're holding back from me because of some idiot that hurt you ten years ago, not because of anything I've done to you! You are a coward!"

"A coward!" The altercation was getting hotter; couples who were looking to join another couple at a table passed them by.

"You arrogant imbecile! I am not a coward. I am not afraid of you. I do want to be cautious because of mistakes in my past and because of Cassie, but that has nothing to do with you. I've held back with you because of the bet and because I'm not the kind of woman to just jump into bed with every man I meet. You chauvinistic, macho nincompoop!"

"The bet was a joke and you know it, you bad-tempered little witch!" Frank was yelling too, then realized that people were listening and lowered his voice. "It was just a friendly push from people who care enough about me to give me a prod so that I'd notice just how wonderful you really are! No one expected me to actually get married just so Kate would have to buy me lunch once a week. How dumb do you think I am? I have my feelings and my dreams too, you know! You want me to care about your dreams and worry about your feelings but you don't seem to give a damn about mine. Have you ever thought about me?" And so it continued.

It was a glorious quarrel. They exchanged verbal barbs with unyielding wrath. Neither one pulled any verbal punches. The dust-up lasted all the way through a very good lunch which they devoured completely without missing a word, and for the whole journey back to the station. Neither of them gave an inch. No one conceded defeat, no winner was declared.

They parted with Frank saying, "I'm glad to be back to civilization where women aren't afraid to be women. Too scared to kiss a man or even to sleep with the man they're involved with."

"Afraid?" Lanie shrieked, still angry. "I think not. That's the bottom line, isn't it? I just didn't sleep with you. I didn't feel ready yet. That's all you really want. What about my feelings? I'm not a damned prize." She lowered her voice dangerously, "And we're not involved. It's not like we're in the middle of a passionate affair; we've shared one kiss. One. It was our first, and it will be our last if I have anything to say about it. No matter how soul shattering it was!" She stalked off, muttering to herself as she got into her car. "Just because he thinks that kiss is going to make me toss and turn all night thinking about it! Huh!"

She heard Frank call after her with laughter in his voice. "Liar! We've had several soul shattering kisses and you do want to sleep with me almost as much as I want to sleep with you. I could see it in your eyes. I could feel it in the way you held me. Hell, I could tell you weren't indifferent just by looking down at your sweater. I could see your--"

"Drop it Buster!" she shot back.

Tina had dropped Lanie's car off in the parking lot since she couldn't be there to pick Lanie up. Lanie set her purse on the hood and dug out her keys. She tossed her suitcases into the back seat and got into the car.

"It's true and you know it. You were as hot as I was. In fact, we would have made love if Caroline hadn't been murdered!" he called with a smile on his face. "You're already falling in love with me and that's really why you're running scared."

"You conceited jackass!" She rolled down her window and yelled out at him, "I'll fall in love with you on a cold day in hell!"

"How about on a warm day in California?" Frank leaned in her window and admitted with his voice lowered, "I'm falling in love too, Lanie, and it scares the heck out of me as well. It also excites me. Let's be scared and excited together." She started her car before she heard him call out again. "Be careful, my love. You know what a bad driver you are when you're um, aroused."

Lanie pulled away from him and maneuvered out of her parking space and drove home very carefully, all too aware that she was mad enough to run little old ladies off the road just for the fun of it. The drive calmed her a little. Part way home some of the things he had said sank in, things she hadn't noticed in the heat of her anger. Phrases like: "a woman I treasure" and "how wonderful you are" and even "I'm falling in love too, Lanie" suddenly came into focus. She was so shocked she pulled the car over to reflect on those phrases. Good glory! Lanie thought, could it possibly be true? Could Frank actually care for her? Genuinely care? She remembered his final phrase, "Let's be scared and excited together." In spite of her anger, the mind numbing thought made her smile. How could you stay mad at a man who said things like that?

Arriving home, she unloaded her suitcases from the car and went into the house to look for Cassie and Tina. They weren't there. On the kitchen table she found a note from Tina telling her that they had gone over to Kate's houses for a swim. The note said to call when she got home.

She called Kate's house. "Hello Kate, this is Lanie. Are Tina and Cassie there?"

"They just left. Cassie swims like she's part fish." Kate could hear the tension in her voice. "You sound upset. Lanie, are you all right?"

"I was furious with Frank when I left the station, now I'm just confused," Lanie confessed, "and I think I probably should be mad at you too now that I think of it. You made a bet on me, on my life. My future. Kate, I am not Secretariat."

"True enough. He was a stallion, but you *are* both redheads. Lanie, that bet is a joke and if you'd admit it, you know that's all it was," Kate told her. "If you and Frank aren't happy together, just don't see each other anymore. It's that simple. Really. But first tell me one thing--was the weekend with Frank all that terrible? Did he make heavy-handed passes at you constantly? Is he stupid? Boring? Rude? A bad dinner companion?"

"No, most of the weekend was okay." She finally relented, "Heck, it was wonderful. Frank was perfect. He didn't make crude passes, he's smart and attentive, and funny. He is fun to talk to."

"And argue with?" Kate interrupted.

"Yes, that too," Lanie admitted. "He had my white dress copied for me. I was very touched by that. He dances superbly.

He even has good table manners."

"Then what's the problem?" Kate asked. "If I weren't happily married, I'd be looking for a man like that. Face it, he's even good-looking."

"Don't give me that. He's much more than good-looking, he is very handsome," Lanie admitted, "and extremely nice, fun to be with and considerate."

"Does he leave you feeling cold? Unaffected?" Kate asked.

"Hell no!" Lanie laughed, "He makes me feel like I'm in an elevator that just dropped twenty floors, or like I'm standing in the path of a hurricane."

"How rude and thoughtless of me to try to set you up with a man like that. I am so sorry. Not," Kate apologized insincerely. "So, once again, what's the problem?"

"He's a jerk!" Lanie exploded. "He's really a wonderful guy but he's a total jerk!"

"Lanie, I know that," Kate reminded her. "He's a man, it's the nature of the beast. The best of them can be wonderful, it's true, but they're still men and sometimes they're also jerks. Remember that."

"Okay, Kate." Lanie laughed. "I'll try to remember that."

"Oh, I doubt he'll let you forget it," Kate said softly.

"I told him to go away and stay away," Lanie admitted. "What if he does?"

"Since when does a man do what you ask him to?" Kate told her, "He'll come up with some lame excuse for you to spend time together and then give you a hard time. All you have to do is make him work hard to get back in your good graces."

"But the fight was my fault," Lanie protested.

"It doesn't matter whose fault it was." Kate waved her protest aside. "First you teach him a lesson, then grab him and don't let go. Lanie, believe me, he's really a good man."

"I know he is," Lanie laughed, "but I'll deny it if you ever repeat it. Kate?"

"What is it?" she asked.

"Part of the problem is that I am afraid to get too involved with someone. I don't know if you know it," her voice dropped, "but Cassie's father was abusive, physically abusive, and he left me as soon as I got pregnant. Heck, we weren't even married, just engaged. The creep only paused long enough to run up bills on all my credit cards and drain our joint bank accounts. Then he got out of Dodge. He's never even seen Cassie. He wanted me to abort her. I don't even know if he's aware that I ever went through with the pregnancy and had her."

"Frank's not like that," Kate said gently. "He would cherish you, not abuse you, and he loves kids. He told me he wants as many as possible."

"I know," Lanie admitted. "I know he's nothing like Cal. But I knew Cal wasn't like that either until the first punch landed."

"It must be hard to open yourself up to love again. It was for me. My fear, with Bob, was completely different than yours, but just as deep and real, and every bit as paralyzing," Kate paused, remembering. "I had lost a husband. Joe was his name. I loved him dearly, and he loved me and treated me like a queen. We had it all: the passion, the humor, and the friendship. We were a team. Losing him was devastating. It was even worse because my children were so young. My fear was of loving and losing again through disease or accident. I never had the fear of being hurt by Bob. I only had the fear that I might have to face that terrible pain again."

"I can understand that. What helped you overcome your fear?" Lanie asked with concern.

"I didn't really. Not completely. I just decided I could have Bob for however long the good Lord gives us or I could go through life without him at all. I couldn't face life without him so I decided to put my trust and our love in God's hands and go for it," Kate told Lanie. "And that's what you'll have to decide for yourself. Is Frank the one you love enough to face all the risks for? Or would your life be better without him? Don't answer me, just think it over."

"Thanks Kate," Lanie said quietly. "You're all right. I'll even forgive you for betting on my love life."

"Right now, I'd bet I'm going to lose," Kate laughed with genuine pleasure, "and lose big time."

Chapter Ten

Lanie said good-bye to Kate and hung up the phone just as she heard a car in the driveway. Very soon after that, Tina and Cassie came in the front door. They swept into the small house with all the calm and subtlety of a minor hurricane, leaving about as much of a mess in their wake. Cassie tossed down her towels and toys, and ran over to Lanie to give her a fierce hug. The little girl smelled faintly of chlorine.

"I'm so glad you're home, Mommy! I missed you a whole lot!" she exclaimed. "Did you and your friend Frank have a really good time? What was it like? Did you solve the mystery? Boy! I'd really like to take a trip on a train someday."

"I missed you too, Sweetie, more than you can ever know." Lanie hugged her daughter back. "Now, put your things away. Run upstairs, shower, change out of that wet swimsuit, and I'll tell you all about it." Cassie bounded up the stairs and Lanie called after her, "After your shower be sure rinse out that wet swimsuit, and bring it downstairs and hang it out to dry!"

Tina hugged Lanie next. "I'd better shower, too. I'm as much of a mess as Cassie. I'll be right down as soon as I'm dressed. You have a few minutes before the Q and A session begins, but I want all the juicy details." Tina headed for the stairs.

Lanie was fidgety, her nerves stretched tight by the time Tina and Cassie returned, but she calmly answered all their questions about the Mystery Train and gave them wild descriptions of the various murders, actors, and other travelers as well as she could. She told them about the comfort of the train, praised the great food, and commended the comfortable inn on the coast. She raved about the Saturday night dinner and dance. She described in glowing terms how it felt to solve the mystery correctly and win the prize.

Of course she had gifts for both of them, a T-shirt with the mystery train logo on the front for Cassie, and some perfume from the Hotel's gift shop for Tina. Throughout all of her descriptions and tall tales, somehow she managed to avoid any mention of Frank.

"Thanks for the T-shirt, Mommy. You didn't tell us about your boyfriend Frank, wasn't he on the train with you?" Cassie asked, full of excitement. "Did you have a lot of fun with him?"

Lanie had known it was too good to last. "What do you mean about Frank?" Lanie asked her daughter, puzzled. "I've never spoken to you about him, and as far as I know you've never met him except at Kate's wedding. Frank's just a friend but he's definitely not my boyfriend. I don't know where you got that idea but you can forget it."

"I'm not stupid Mommy, I know you got all those notes from him," Cassie told her, sounding surprisingly worldly for a nine-year-old girl. "And all of those gifts. There was fancy perfume and bracelets and earrings and lacy panties and pearls and--"

"I know what my secret admirer sent me, Cassie." Lanie stopped the recitation firmly.

"But Mommy! He must be really neat if he sent you all those things. Aunt Tina agrees with me that he's really hot, and a sure-enough handsome hunk and she even said that if I'm lucky he'll be my new daddy," Cassie protested.

"Aunt Tina talks too much for her own good." Lanie muttered under her breath, "A sure-enough handsome hunk, indeed! Where would you even hear a phrase like that? It sounds like something your Grandma would say." Lanie shot her sister a narrow-eyed look as she continued talking to Cassie. "Do you even know what hot means? Frank is a nice man and he is very handsome, too. But that's all. I don't even know when I'll see him again. We had a fight just before I got home. It was a very bad argument. Of course, there is still a very real chance we might make up and I would start to see him again." She paused. "However, sweetie, if things ever start to look like there's even a remote chance that he would be your new father, I'll make sure you two spend some time together and get to know each other a lot better. You'll have a say in it before he becomes your daddy, but that's a long way off, okay?"

"Okay," Cassie persisted, "but I'd like a real Daddy."

After Cassie ran outside to play, Tina cornered Lanie. "What happened between you and Frank anyway? Anything good?"

"We had fun and there is an attraction there, but that's all it is." Lanie paused. "Just before I came home we had a fight."

"Before the fight, was there any good stuff?" Tina persisted.

"Not the kind you're thinking of," Lanie said firmly, "but we did get to know each other more. We relaxed and had fun together. We talked a lot. But so far there's only been a few kisses between us. Great kisses. Spectacular kisses, but that's all that happened. And then we argued."

"What happened?" Tina asked with concern.

"He was provoking me but I really picked the fight, I don't even know why." Lanie admitted, "Maybe I panicked. My feelings for him scare me. It's been so long since I felt like this."

"But it's worth it, isn't it?" Tina prodded. "The chance you have to take to be happy."

"Yes. It is." Lanie smiled softly. "You want to know something weird? In the middle of our fight, when he was furious with me, he said he wanted to treat me like a woman he treasured. In the middle of the fight," she shook her head and smiled gently, "now that's what I call fighting dirty."

"Maybe that's how you should treat him," Tina suggested. "Like a man you treasure. It seems to me more relationships would survive if both parties followed that rule."

"I'll think it over," Lanie said softly.

Over the next few weeks there were no more secret admirer notes. In fact there were no phone calls, not even a single word from Frank of any kind. Nothing at all. Lanie knew it was irrational, given their angry parting, but she had never felt so abandoned or so irritated in her life. She felt like she'd been cast aside like a pair of torn pantyhose. She wanted to hear from him. She wanted to apologize. She wanted revenge. Heck, she wanted him!

She was working at her drafting board in her stark, white office one day trying to design the layout for an extensive garden when she finally heard from him. The company receptionist, an older woman named Mary, took a message from Frank asking Lanie to contact him at her earliest convenience. Mary hand delivered the message to Lanie.

"Is this business or is it personal, Lanie?" Mary asked, unrepentantly curious. "I hope it's personal. He sounds very handsome to me. You need a personal life."

"What I need," Lanie returned quietly, looking at the gray haired woman with a mixture of humor and exasperation, "is a receptionist who'll get the man on the line for me, please. It doesn't matter if it's business or personal if I can't talk to him, does it? And besides, how can a man sound handsome?"

"He just did." Returning to her desk in a mild huff, Mary dialed the number on the note, worked her way through a receptionist at Frank's office and finally reached Frank.

"I have a call for you from Ms. McPherson, please hold." She buzzed Lanie and said stiffly, "I have your call on line three."

"Hi Lanie. How's it going?" Frank sounded disgustingly cheerful. "Are you still mad at me?"

"Always." Lanie tried to sound stern. "What's up?" She heard a snicker from the receiver and she was instantly glad he couldn't see her sudden blush. "I mean, what do you want?"

"That question is almost as bad. I want world peace, lots of money, your company's services to landscape my new house, and about a century in bed with you. Not necessarily in that order," Frank told her.

"I can't create world peace but I would if I could. You can get your own darn money, and how much is lots anyway? However, I can have someone from my firm do the landscaping at your new home. That's no problem. By the way, what new house? And finally, dream on buddy, you haven't got a prayer of getting anywhere near a bed with me in this century or any other," Lanie replied firmly. "For any amount of time."

"I want you, not just somebody from your firm," Frank said decisively. "I want your services."

"For your landscaping job?" she asked suspiciously.

"Of course." He paused. "For a start."

"Okay. Give me your address and I'll go by and look over the property, then I'll meet with you and we can discuss what you have in mind," Lanie suggested. "For me."

She was slightly rattled at the thought of seeing him again. The advice from Kate had been swirling around in her brain. "I mean we can discuss your preferences," she paused when he laughed softly, "about what landscaping ideas you have."

"Better yet, I'll pick you up and we can discuss my ideas and yours while you look at the property," Frank suggested.

"Okay," Lanie agreed quickly without any argument.

"Lanie? You're being suspiciously agreeable all of a sudden," Frank observed.

"Don't worry about it." She laughed softly, "It's a phase. I can guarantee you it won't last."

She was curiously content when she hung up the phone. In fact she was so happy, she made a special effort to soothe Mary's ruffled feathers.

About an hour later Frank picked her up at her office. As she left with him she noticed Mary making a circle with her thumb and forefinger in a gesture meaning okay, as she nodded at Frank.

Together they drove to his new house just outside the edge of town. The air was electric between them. It was filled with a combination of nervous energy and sexual tension. Even though they just had a good conversation over the phone, the last time they had actually seen each other they had fought and fought hard. Some of the tension was still there, almost like a static barrier in the air between them, keeping them apart. The barrier broke when Lanie groaned as she saw Frank's new house.

It was, to put it mildly, a fixer-upper. The house needed external repairs and paint. It was two stories, large and rambling. Several of the windows needed to be replaced. The screen door was off its hinges. The front porch sagged.

To top it all off, the house was covered with chipped and flaky dull, gray paint. The large, surrounding yard was a mess, all the land was either bare dirt or completely overgrown with weeds. Frank told her the whole property was just over three acres in total.

"What do you think of it?" Frank asked excitedly.

"You've already bought this?" Lanie requested cautiously.

"Yes. Isn't it neat?" Frank had all the enthusiasm of a first time homeowner.

"No Frank, it isn't neat, it's a mess," Lanie told him honestly. "It's going to be a lot of time and work to fix it up, not to mention a huge expense. That is, if it's even structurally sound."

"It is. I had an inspection. I'm not a total fool," he told her. "And the inside of the house isn't nearly as bad as the outside. The inside is livable right now, except that I have some remodeling I want to do before I move in."

"Thank goodness for small favors." Lanie began to sketch the yard and the exterior of the house, walking around and occasionally measuring distances. "Frank? What kind of ideas do you have for this place?"

"I want a large front lawn with a good sprinkler system. I also want a flowerbed and some shrubs around the house. Along the property line I want a few trees, maybe some fruit trees.

Eventually I'm going to put a pool in the backyard and a play area, so I'll want a good, high sturdy fence around each of those." He was talking off the top of his head and she knew it, but the feelings behind his half-formed ideas were real. "I might even put a barn in the back and a corral for a few horses."

"I have enough for now to draw up a few ideas. I'll formulate them and then give you a few suggestions for your choices of grass, shrubs, flowers, and trees."

"Lanie, while you're here would you like to see my house? The inside, I mean," Frank asked, almost pleading. "Please?"

"I'd love to." She couldn't help smiling at his eagerness.

Just like Frank had said, the house was in better shape inside than outside. The kitchen and dining room were both large, open areas. However the appliances did need to be replaced. There was a separate laundry room off the kitchen, and a large pantry. All these rooms needed was paint and having the floors refurbished. A small, formal sitting room, an entryway, a living room, a family room, and a tiny bathroom completed the downstairs. Upstairs, there were four large bedrooms and another bathroom.

"I thought I'd make two of the bedrooms into one really nice master bedroom with it's own bath, sitting room, and a walk-in closet," Frank told her. "Then I'd polish the hardwood floors and paint the two smaller bedrooms and paint and retile the other bathroom."

"And downstairs?" Lanie asked, interested almost against her will.

"Downstairs I want to modernize the kitchen and dining areas, and then just open up all the rest of the area for a wide open living space." He grinned. "Except for the bathroom, of course. The whole house needs to be painted inside, and the hardwood floors needs sanding."

"It sounds like a great home for a family," Lanie said as they walked downstairs. "But it sounds a bit too much for a single guy like you."

"Haven't you heard?" Frank was only partly teasing her. "I'll be a family man real soon. I'm planning on getting married within the next year."

"Don't bet on it."

"I already did. Lanie?" Frank asked. "Want to explore the basement with me? I haven't been down there yet."

"Okay." She grinned.

Frank open the door. "After you."

"No, after you." She laughed. "I don't trust those stairs."

She followed him down the creaky stairs, dodging cobwebs. Frank found a light switch. Once lit, the basement was dusty with a few abandoned belongings and lots of cobwebs. They just reached the bottom of the steps when they heard the door slam above them. Suddenly, they wanted to get out of there. They climbed the stairs but soon learned they couldn't open the door.

"No one knows where we are." Frank tried to break down the door but it was surprisingly solid.

"Mary knows where I am. Tina will come find me if I don't pick up Cassie." Lanie looked around and found some old camping gear. "Let's relax and wait to be rescued."

She handed him an old air mattress. "Here, put that hot air of yours to some good use."

She shook an old sleeping bag, then laid it over the stair rail and beat it with an abandoned golf club. It raised a cloud of musty dust. She carried it over to where Frank had the mattress, near a window that was too small and too high for them to use to get out. However he had managed to open it and let in some fresh air. She put the sleeping bag on the mattress and they both laid down. They talked for a short time, then began moving closer to each other. They began kissing, first soft and tender but soon sizzling, hard kisses, devouring each other. Frank started to pull Lanie's tank top over her head when Lanie's cell phone rang.

"You had a cell phone on you the whole time?" Frank raised

himself up on one elbow. "I thought we were trapped."

"Shh!" Lanie answered her cell. "Hello Tina."

She sat up, alert. "How bad?"

She gave the address and directions. "Tina, we're trapped in the basement. Open the door in the kitchen but don't come down the stairs."

Lanie's voice was calm but Frank knew something had upset her. "What's up?

"Cassie fell off a swing and cut her forehead. It's not bad but she may need stitches, and she's a little groggy. "Lanie started to stand. "Tina's coming to get me and we're taking her to a doctor."

"We have a few minutes then, so try to relax." Frank gently pulled her back down to the mattress.

He enfolded her in his arms, offering comfort. She did relax, knowing Tina would have called an ambulance if Cassie were really hurt. She snuggled closer to Frank and her comfort increased. She lifted her face to Frank. It was all the invitation he needed. He kissed her, teasing and coaxing a sweet response from her. His lips were marvelous, firm and soft. His tongue danced in her mouth. His hands roamed gently over the curves of her body. It went on and on until they heard Tina clearing her throat.

"Sorry to interrupt, guys, but I have Cassie in the car and I really think she should go to the E.R. sometime soon." She stood at the top of the stairs.

Chapter Eleven

"Hi Tina, I'm ready to go," Lanie told Tina as she broke away from Frank. "Is Cassie out in the car?"

"Yes, she is," Tina said.

"How is she?" Lanie asked.

"She seems a bit groggy," Tina told her.

Lanie started up the stairs.

"Hey wait!" Frank said as he recovered from his romantic fog. "I'm coming, too."

Lanie looked back over her shoulder. "You don't have to, you hardly even know Cassie."

Frank met her gaze squarely and replied, "That's right. I don't even know Cassie very well yet but I'm still coming along. I don't even know your sister Tina at all yet, but I soon will."

"I can take a hint. Tina this is Frank, Frank this is Tina." She gestured as she made the sparse introductions.

"Pleased to meet you, Tina." Frank offered his hand. "I think we're going to get to know each other real well."

"I think we are too. You look just like I pictured you from Lanie's description," Tina told him.

"That's funny," Frank was pleased, "I thought she'd describe me as a clumsy jerk."

"I do seem to recall those words being mentioned once or twice but there were other words mentioned along with them." Tina laughed.

"What other words?" Frank prodded gently, curious.

"Words like tall, blonde and gorgeous," Tina grinned, "along with a great smile and a good sense of humor."

"Tina!" Lanie was spurred into instant action to shut her

sister up. "Shut up you traitor. We have to leave, now!"

Frank followed the sisters to the nearest hospital in his own car. Lanie had already carried Cassie into the busy waiting room by the time he got his car parked in the crowded hospital parking lot. He joined them in the emergency waiting room. Cassie was drowsy and a little fussy. She had a bandage loosely covering a long, slashing cut across her cheek, and a badly scraped elbow.

Lanie had gently put the injured little girl in a waiting room chair near the reception desk. Frank walked over to stand beside the little girl who could be his future daughter. He just wanted to stand close to her. He wasn't going to disturb her since she seemed sleepy and there would be plenty of time to really get to know her later.

Cassie wasn't as drowsy as she looked however. She wasn't too drowsy to say, "Hi, Frank, I remember you. We met at that funny wedding. Do you remember me? I'm Cassie."

Frank knelt down to look at the little girl eye to eye. "Yes, of course I remember you from the wedding. I'm very glad to see you again, Cassie. I'm sorry you hurt your head."

"Are you my Mommy's boyfriend?" she asked. "Whenever I ask her that she gets a real funny look on her face and she never, ever answers me. Will you tell me?"

"Yes Cassie, I'll answer you. I sure am your Mommy's boyfriend," he told her. "She just hasn't admitted it yet, not even to herself."

"Why?" Cassie's little face looked puzzled.

"Because she's afraid of being hurt." Frank told the girl gently, "It's like if you had a very best friend and she decided she liked someone else and stopped talking to you. That would hurt you, wouldn't it?"

"Yes," Cassie nodded.

"But I'll never do that to your mother, I promise." Frank smiled at the little girl. "I hope I'll be your friend always, too."

"Good." Her little voice trailed off. "We can be friends. I

like you."

Frank was genuinely touched by the childish statement and by the open honesty of the little girl. Tina and Frank watched over the drowsy child while Lanie checked in with the E.R. receptionist, showing her proof of insurance and filling out the endless hospital forms.

Cassie roused herself again before very long. She stirred just enough to start complaining about her face. She said that it hurt but she didn't want to see a doctor and she sure didn't want to get any shots. She was quite definite on that point, no shots!

"I know what you mean, I don't like seeing doctors either, not at all. And I really hate shots, but the doctor will stop your face from hurting so much and he will make sure it heals like it should without leaving any scars." Frank smiled then tried to distract her. "I like the frog on your T-shirt."

Cassie had on red shorts and a red t-shirt with a big green frog appliqué on the front of it. Frank sat down in the chair beside her and told her a silly, funny story about a pet frog named Willie. Willie liked to watch talk shows from his aquarium while his owner took her afternoon nap. He also liked watching game shows almost more than catching flies. Lanie finished with the receptionist and paced while listening to Frank's silly, touching story and waiting for Cassie's turn to be seen by a doctor.

Finally a harried woman in hospital greens called for Cassie to go into an exam room. Lanie started to carry her in. Suddenly Cassie was fully awake and rebellious.

"I want Frank to come too!" the little girl protested, struggling. "He was telling me about Willie the frog."

At a nod from the nurse, he followed them into a small curtained off cubicle with a bed, leaving Tina alone in the waiting area.

There was another wait once they got Cassie undressed and into the bed. The nurse took Cassie's vital signs and told them that the hospital had already called a plastic surgeon to do the sutures on Cassie's face because they wanted to be sure there were no scars.

"Is that really necessary?" Lanie asked, worried. "Is it that bad?"

"Not really, but it should take a couple of stitches. The plastic surgeon was just leaving his office when we called and said he'd come in. We just don't want to leave any scars on that beautiful little face," the nurse reassured her. "Would you?"

"Of course not." Lanie relaxed a bit.

When Cassie dozed off, Frank went out to the waiting room to let Tina know what was happening. With Cassie and Lanie both out of her sight, Frank noticed how nervous and upset Tina seemed to be. He quickly searched for something to say to distract Tina.

"Nice outfit, that black and blue sweater looks great with those black slacks," he said rather lamely.

"It's just an old outfit I use for things like playing in the park with Cassie." Tina seemed dispirited.

Frank tried again, "This hospital seems fairly nice, as hospitals go." He grinned. "At least the colors are cheerful and the chairs are fairly comfortable. I remember when hospital waiting rooms seemed to be made as deliberately uncomfortable and unattractive as possible, as if to encourage people to get up and leave."

"It may look better than it used to but I would still rather not be here," Tina told him tensely. "Damn! I hate it when she's hurt."

"So? What happened to her? How did she get hurt?" Frank asked gently as he put his arm around her shoulder. "Tell me about it."

"She fell off the swings in the park and the seat came back and hit her in the face. For a minute it looked like she was going to lose consciousness but she didn't. She does seem sort of groggy though," Tina told him, fighting back tears. "I hope she doesn't get a scar. I always feel so responsible, so guilty, if she gets hurt while I'm watching her."

"Hey! She's an active nine-year-old. It would be really strange if she didn't get hurt occasionally." Frank gave Tina a quick reassuring hug. "No matter who's watching her."

"Now that I feel a bit better, tell me about that little scene I saw in the basement. I take it Lanie's not mad at you anymore." Tina relaxed a little and managed a weak grin for Frank. "She sure didn't look angry to me."

"Believe it or not, for most of the time we were down there we only talked," Frank told her. "We talked about everything and anything. It was our longest and most, um, intimate conversation ever. We needed it. We needed to really get to know each other. We didn't even start kissing until after you called. Tina, I'm still stunned by one thing."

"What?" Tina pushed.

"Tina, she never told me she had a phone in her pocket. I don't know what would have happened if you hadn't called." Frank ran one hand through his wavy, thick hair. "Pardon me if I seem a bit distracted, but it was looking real promising for a moment down there."

"She wouldn't have stayed down there much longer, no matter what happened," Tina told him, beaming. "If it got to the point where she'd be late for dinner she would have called us. She'd never let Cassie worry."

"Still, it was the first time she's ever shown me that she even wanted to be in the same room with me. I mean we enjoyed ourselves on the Mystery Train, but we were thrown together and there wasn't any choice. This time, in the basement, she could have easily walked away and instead, she chose to stay with me," Frank told Tina. As he put his thoughts into words he realized, "It's a good sign."

"Considering how that rat Cal treated her and the emotional scars she got from him, it's a great sign," Tina confirmed.

"So how's *your* love life?" Frank turned the tables on her.

"I'm doing better than Lanie was before she met you, but not much better," Tina grinned, with irony in her voice. "I date occasionally, but there's no one man that I'd really miss if I never saw him again."

"Sometimes that's even worse than not dating at all. I've been there," Frank told her. "Talk to Kate and Laura."

"Maybe I will and maybe I won't. I want someone to date that I could care about but I'm not sure I want to get married yet," Tina said. "Those two are lethal. It's even more frightening when they work together. I've never seen them fail."

With a reassuring squeeze to Tina's hand, Frank went back in to check on Cassie. Upon entering the room he found that the doctor had arrived and was just about to give Cassie a local anesthetic before putting in a few very fine and delicate stitches.

While the local was being injected in several places under Cassie's delicate skin, Frank held her hand and told her more stories about Willie the frog and his friend Larry the lizard. He talked about how Larry liked to get out of the aquarium and hide, and then he'd jump out scaring all the visitors who came to see his owner. Larry was a very bad lizard but his owner loved him anyway.

The doctor quickly put a few very fine stitches in Cassie's face and covered them with a bandage. He then cleaned and dressed Cassie's scraped elbow. He checked the chart and took Cassie's vital signs again. Then he gave Lanie explicit instructions to wake her every two hours and talk to her to make sure she was coherent. The he sent her home.

"I'd admit her for observation but her vital signs are normal and I believe you'll take very good care of her and she will rest better at home," the doctor said. "Just bring her back if you see any problems. Watch her for forty-eight hours and take her to her own doctor as soon as possible. Call my office for an appointment to remove the stitches." He gave her a card.

Lanie picked up Cassie to carry her out but Frank went to her and took the sleeping child from her arms.

"She's a big girl, let me carry her," Frank offered.

He carried Cassie out to the car and put her in the back seat, fastening a seatbelt around the little girl and covering her with a blanket. Tina drove while Lanie sat in the back beside Cassie. Frank followed them in his own car. In spite of the injured child, he was a little excited. It was the first chance he would have to see Lanie's home.

"I have to stay with her tonight," Lanie told Frank as she watched him carry Cassie into the house. "She's drowsy because of the blow to her head; it might be a slight concussion. The doctor said I should watch her very closely tonight. He was very encouraging about her cheek. He said it wouldn't scar."

"She is going to need her mother here when she wakes up," Frank finished for her. "Why don't you go take a quick shower while I fix us all something to eat?"

"You may be a truly nice man after all," Lanie said softly.

"You don't have to sound so surprised. I told you that all along." Frank touched her gently on the cheek.

Neither one of them noticed that Tina had slipped away, leaving them alone. Lanie showered while Frank got busy in the small, gleaming kitchen. He searched the refrigerator and started dinner. He made a salad, put some potatoes in the microwave, and got some steaks ready to grill. When Lanie came into the kitchen in clean black shorts and a soft pink T-shirt, Frank went in to wash up as well as he could, getting the basement grime off, without a change of clothes.

By the time he returned the steaks were ready and they could sit down and eat. Lanie had opened a bottle of red wine. She was still a bit worried about Cassie, and only half-heartedly pecked at her food. Frank noticed her lack of appetite and decided to change things, shake her up, just a little bit.

"Hey lady," he teased, "I worked hard on that dinner. I had to tear up some lettuce and wash two whole potatoes." His eyes narrowed. "You better eat it or I'm gonna have to get tough with you."

"Tough?" One eyebrow arched cynically.

"You do know what happens to bad little girls who don't eat all their dinner, don't you?" he asked threateningly.

"Yeah," she deadpanned, "they stay thin."

"And they don't get dessert," he told her.

"Did you make any dessert?" she asked.

"No," he admitted.

"So?" she challenged back. "What else happens to bad little girls who don't eat their dinner?"

"Sometimes the cook puts them over his knee and gives them a real hard spanking." He grinned, noticing that as they talked, she began to eat a little.

"And sometimes the cook winds up with a knee in his groin and walks funny for a week." She raised her eyebrows again, wiggling them at him defiantly.

"I'm going to wash these dishes before I leave," Frank said, reluctantly standing up. "You just keep eating your dinner."

"Are you're leaving?" She was surprised. "Somehow I thought you'd want to stay and--"

"I'm leaving," Frank said firmly, "but I'll be right back. Not to continue anything we were doing in the cellar but because I want to help you with Cassie. How can you get any sleep if you have to wake her every two hours?"

"You're coming over to help me care for Cassie but not anything else?" she pushed for clarification.

"There are rules, Lanie," he explained softly. "One of them is that you don't make a pass at a woman who's worried sick about an injured child."

"Really?" Lanie was mildly surprised.

"But as soon as she's feeling better, lady," he whispered close to her ear, "you'd better run."

"What if I don't want to run? ARGH!" Just as she started to

reply with her question it happened, Frank bumped into her wine glass and spilled it all over her lap. He quickly handed her some paper towels before he finished gathering up dishes.

"What are you?" She laughed. "An undercover employee of the dry cleaner's association? In charge of sales for the paper towel manufacturer's of the western world? Or just a total klutz?"

"I've never been a klutz around any other woman but you," he kissed her on the cheek before starting to wash the dishes, "my love."

True to his word, Frank went home, showered, changed into sweats and then came back. Lanie had already checked on Cassie once, so he sent her to bed with her alarm set for four hours. He set his travel alarm for two hours and stretched out on the sofa.

Later that night as she slept alone and tossed restlessly, his sentence ran over and over through her brain along with two burning questions: Did it mean she really was special to him? Did he really mean to call her "my love?"

Around two AM she heard Frank as he climbed the stairs and checked on Cassie. She called out to him as he left the girl's room.

"Frank?" she called softly. "Don't take this as a pass or anything but you can come in here with me if you want to. You can't get any rest on that sofa. It's far too short for you"

Frank grinned as he got into the bed beside Lanie, still wearing his sweats. It wasn't the way he had envisioned his first night in bed with Lanie, but a starving man makes a feast out of crumbs.

He awoke the next morning with Lanie in his arms. At some point during the night he'd removed his sweats, so he only had on an undershirt and his shorts. He laid there for a short time holding Lanie before he got up to check on Cassie. The little girl was fine except for being a bit grouchy about having someone wake her every two hours and ask her stupid questions.

Frank quickly showered, shaved and dressed for the day. He looked into Lanie's refrigerator and noticed that she had everything he would need to fix her a great breakfast. He mixed some pancake batter, set the table, and got out the butter and syrup. He heard a noise from Lanie's room so he put on the coffee and started frying the bacon. Before long he had pancakes on the griddle, bacon drying on a towel, eggs ready to fry, and orange juice poured.

Lanie entered the kitchen, looked over the breakfast and smiled shyly at Frank. "You really are the most remarkable man!"

"I've been telling you that." He pulled out a chair for her. "You just refuse to believe me."

They sat and enjoyed their breakfasts, then Frank had to leave. He had to get to the office. He was a bit disappointed that he didn't get to say good-bye to Cassie but she was still asleep.

As he left, Frank grabbed Lanie in a tight embrace and said, "I've got to uphold my evil reputation, you understand?"

Lanie nodded silently. Her eyes were big and round and her breath seemed to be coming slowly and very deeply.

Frank kissed her. The kiss started out gently but it soon deepened. Time stopped. Lightening flashed. Tongues met and dueled. They kissed her each other fiercely enough to cause her knees to weaken before Frank left on legs that seemed shaky, too.

Frank was out of town on a business trip for most of the next week. He was tied up in meetings at corporate headquarters most of the time so he didn't have time to call Lanie for several days. When he did, they avoided talking about their budding relationship; instead they talked casually about his trip, her daughter and her injury, and the landscaping work that was being done at his new house.

She told him that Cassie was fine, and the doctor repeated that he didn't expect the cut on her face to leave a permanent scar. He told her that corporate headquarters was boring and very political but the promotion he had been hoping for was official, he was now head of all retail and wholesale sales for the entire West Coast.

She told him that the work remodeling his house had begun, the walls had been knocked down both upstairs and downstairs where rooms were being enlarged. The debris had been hauled away and the construction of the new rooms was ready to be started. In fact the crew was already working on the master bedroom upstairs.

She also told him that they were digging the trenches to place the sprinklers and the holes to plant the trees the next day, plus grading the property. He said he would see her as soon as possible. Both of them were unsatisfied and restless when the short call was over.

Chapter Twelve

Surprisingly, Frank had some good luck the day after he made the last phone call. He finished all of his business at corporate headquarters much sooner than he had originally expected to, and he was able to catch an early flight home on Thursday instead of being stuck there until Saturday. He got into LAX around noon, and flew to John Wayne Airport by two in the afternoon. He had left his car and keys with Laura, so he called her to pick him up at the airport. She suggested having Lanie drive out to the airport but he wanted to surprise her.

Truth be told, Laura was happy to get away from the office a little early so she was waiting for him when he came out pulling his luggage cart. He loaded his suitcases into the trunk and dropped Laura off at her house. He pulled up to his new house shortly after three that afternoon.

His good luck continued because Lanie was still there as he turned his car onto his block. He could see her working in his yard wearing shorts and a tight T-shirt. It looked like she was digging something with a shovel as he pulled up to the newly graded driveway that led up to his house.

Before he turned into the driveway he sat in his car and watched her for a minute, relishing all the emotions that poured over him at the sight of her. He had a real sense of promise and anticipation. She seemed to be working very hard even though she was alone. It looked like the rest of her landscaping crew had already gone home for the day.

His good luck changed abruptly, and when it did, his good mood vanished just as quickly. He wasn't watching where he was going as he pulled his car into the drive. Preoccupied with seeing

Lanie again, he took his eyes off the newly curved driveway and didn't notice that the freshly graded path was slick with mud. He didn't even notice the yellow tape blocking off part of his old driveway, which had been dug up so that it could be planted and become part of the new landscaping.

Actually, he didn't notice any of these things until his car fishtailed on the slick, muddy surface and went off the drive and got stuck in the mud. As he looked out the windshield the driver's side looked like it was muddier than the other side, so he got out of his car on the passenger side and barely avoided sinking up to his knees in the thick, gooey mud.

It wasn't all his fault, not really. It wasn't anybody's fault. His simple joy and anticipation at seeing Lanie faded, and the frustration and weariness set in. Her patience was also at an end. She was buffaloed at the whole mess, trying to fix a mistake that somebody else made.

He was exhausted from the trip and also from what had seemed like dozens of long, boring meetings. She was frustrated, tired, dirty and muddy. He was hungry because he refused to eat the airplane food. She hadn't had time to eat because of the obvious problems at the job site. He was shocked that the water had been turned on in the first place at the house. She was hot and every muscle ached. He was tired and stiff from the confines of the plane. She was irate that she had to send her men home causing them to lose part of their wages and putting her work behind schedule, not to mention the expense her firm would have to eat while trying to fix the muddy mess.

She was already mad at the man who'd dug in the wrong place. He hadn't even had time to change after his last business meeting so he was still wearing an expensive three-piece business suit, a tie, and his best leather shoes instead of his usual casual slacks and T-shirt. She was afraid of Frank's reaction. She knew Frank would blame her for the mess and she was trying desperately to get it cleaned up before he ever saw it.

To top it all off, unfortunately for Lanie there was no way she could hide the mess from Frank. He was already sinking to mid-calf in the mud. Mud that shouldn't have been there. Mud that meant someone had broken a main water pipe. His temper exploded, and hers wasn't far behind.

Instead of the tender, loving greeting he had planned to give Lanie, something entirely different came out when he opened his mouth.

"What in the holy hell is going on here?" he roared. "I thought you were a professional. I thought you had the experience to check and find out where the water pipes were before you started to dig!"

"We did check!" Lanie fired back. Her temper and nerves were frayed to the breaking point; still she tried to hold onto the last bit of temper. "I'm not an idiot! The survey I got from the city must be wrong somehow, not to mention that I had to hire someone new who I'd never used before to do the digging with the backhoe. The man I usually hire to dig the trenches had to be rushed to the hospital with a bad appendix and the operation was yesterday. The new guy was not only an idiot, but he was also a chauvinistic jerk. He ignored everything I said because I'm just a woman. I actually heard him say that to one of my regular men. I would have fired him on the spot but I wanted to get the digging done today. Then he misread the survey, as bad as it was, and dug in the wrong place. Even so, there should still have been plenty of margin for error." She stopped herself and took a deep breath before continuing, "I'm sorry Frank. I can't explain it, the survey must be off."

"Sure." The tone held no conviction at all. Frank pulled off his suit jacket and tossed it onto his car. It landed on top of his trunk. "Well, your firm will make this good at no expense to me, I hope." His tone brooked no argument. His vest and tie followed his jacket onto the car.

"Of course we'll take care of it. What else could we do?"

Lanie was getting mad herself now. "We are a reliable firm. And I will prove to you that this wasn't all my fault. You're such a jerk!" Her eyes flashed. "What in the heck do you think you are doing?"

Frank was unbuttoning his crisp white shirt. "What does it look like? I'm undressing. Why should I get mud on the few clothes that have survived the flood so far?"

He used his shirt to wrap up his watch, his wallet and his imported leather belt, then he tossed the bundle onto the trunk of his car with the rest of his clothes.

"Now, I'll see if there's anything that can be done to control this mess. It looks like I got here just in time." He shot her a glance. "I only wish that saying on your T-shirt was true but it looks like you blew it, doesn't it?"

Lanie looked down at her T-shirt; it was a muddy wet mess but the saying printed across her chest was still readable: **THE BEST MAN FOR THE JOB . . . IS A WOMAN!** She pulled off her shoes and socks. Then, the survey firmly in one hand, she made her way over to him very carefully, trying to avoid the mud as much as possible. She was struggling to hold onto her last vestiges of control.

"Before you wade too deep in that horse pucky you're dishing out, Buster, take a long look at the official survey." Her words were heated, her own volatile temper barely under control. "Do it now or your own words will sink you much deeper than that mud you're standing in!"

She hit him in the chest with the survey. In a lightning move he grabbed her arm and pulled her into the mud next to him. Suddenly, without even looking at the survey, he knew she was right. He knew it from the barely controlled rage on her face.

"Lanie, I'm really sorry." He reached up to stroke her gently on the cheek, not realizing that his hand had somehow become muddy. "I was just tired and hot, and I took everything out on you. Forgive me, please."

"Yeah, sure." Lanie's voice was saccharine sweet as she replied, "Yell at me, get me muddy, call me incompetent and insult my professionalism. Then all you have to do is say, 'sorry, forgive me, I was tired,' and I'm supposed to melt and forgive you? Well, it doesn't quite work that way, Buddy. I'm hot and tired and frustrated, too."

Lanie pulled away from him with much effort. She staggered as she finally broke free of his grip. She dropped to her hands and knees in the mud. It was her breaking point. Frank instantly reached out and took hold of her elbow to help her up. She straightened up all right, struggling and flailing her hands in the mud as she sought to regain her balance. She rose with both hands full. Frank never saw it until it was too late. She pelted him in the face with a handful of mud, barely taking care to avoid his eyes. Frank had started to rein in his temper but it was still near the surface, and getting pelted with mud set it off again.

The fight that followed was very short and not too sweet. It started with mud flying everywhere like a dirty snowball fight, and soon sank to a wrestling match in the wettest, sloppiest part of the large pool of mud. Somehow her T-shirt got torn to the point where it was hanging from her in shreds. Swearing, she pulled the tatters off revealing what had once been a sexy hot pink nylon bra. Determined to get revenge she ripped the button off of his good suit slacks.

"You want my pants, you got 'em! It's your fault they're ruined anyway." Frank managed to stand, unzipped his zipper and stepped out of the ruined slacks, revealing a very muddy pair of bright red jockey shorts.

"Jockeys, huh?" she taunted, standing to face him nose to nose. "I thought you'd be more of a boxer man myself. You seem all wrong for jockey shorts."

"What wrong with jockeys?" Neither one of them was entirely reasonable at the moment. "Or is it me you're trying to insult?"

"Of course it's you I'm insulting, there's nothing wrong with jockeys, nothing at all." Lanie shouted a bit irrationally, "They're just what I should have expected from someone who claims he believes me one minute and then blames me again the next."

Lanie tackled him and brought him back to the ground. She wouldn't have managed it even with a great deal of effort and help from the bad footing of the mud, except for the fact that his balance was ruined by the pants which had fallen down around his knees, tripping him. Attacking furiously, she pulled the ruined pants right off him. He started to retaliate. Just as he managed to get her tight shorts halfway off, almost pulling her underpants off with them, they heard a noise behind them.

"Well, hello there, you two." A gruff voice came from behind them. "This is certainly entertaining but before this fight goes any farther I feel I should let you both know that you're not alone."

They both turned their heads at the words. What they saw made them both groan. Frank covered Lanie with his body before he looked up. Lanie was shaking with laughter.

"Hello, officers," he said calmly, trying not to laugh. "You may have heard this before but this isn't what it looks like. Would you believe we're practicing for a mud-wrestling exhibition?"

"No. Of course it's not what it looks like, it never is. We had a report of possible vandalism and domestic violence," the taller of two police officers said in a flat monotone voice.

"It's not vandalism, it just looks like a mess. I was landscaping and a water pipe broke, causing this mess. It's also not domestic violence, officer, I just want to kill him, that's all," Lanie said with a genuine laugh. "He's blaming me for all this mud."

"And who's landscaping firm dug into an old water pipe and caused the mud?" Frank pointed out, the two police officers momentarily forgotten. "You and your firm are to blame for all this mud."

"I'll need to see some identification from both of you." The policeman didn't seem amused. "Miss, you go explain everything to the other officer while I take this man's statement."

The other officer was a blond female with an athletic build and an air of understanding and sympathy, which was why she was especially good at handling domestic violence. After looking at Lanie's identification and hearing Lanie's tale of the fight, she glanced over at her male partner. He seemed involved in talking to Frank; in fact the two men were laughing together. Both of them avoided looking over at Lanie. The policewoman quietly moved so that her back was to the men.

"Take my advice, Ma'am," she said softly, "make him pay for this big time, but *after* you share a long, hot shower together. This ought to be good for a nice dinner, flowers and maybe even more."

"Officer!" Lanie protested with shock. "Shower together? Our relationship isn't like that . . . I mean we haven't even--. Not ever."

"So? What are you waiting for?" She winked. "Grab the man. You don't find men like that every day. He's a hunk. Trust me. I'm a trained investigator working on becoming a detective and I can detect a hunk from half a mile away, even if he isn't half-naked."

All of a sudden Lanie was suspicious of this policewoman. Something alerted her instincts. "Officer, you don't know happen to know Laura Kelsey or Kate Simmons do you?"

"The matchmakers?" She grinned as she turned to walk back to her partner. "I never heard of either one of them before the night they introduced me to a man named Alan. That was about eight months ago."

"What happened?" Lanie asked, half fearing the answer.

"Alan's my husband now." The officer turned her attention back to Lanie and grinned.

"I'm doomed," Lanie moaned.

"And you love it, almost as much as you love him." The female officer left Lanie to join her partner, but turned back to add, "By the way, Ma'am, you really should pull those shorts back up."

Just then, Frank came over to Lanie. "They've decided not to charge you with anything. Thanks to me." The police officers got into a squad car and drove away.

"Charge me?" Lanie's voice rose. "For what?

"For the vandalism, the assault on me, or even for the indecent exposure," Frank said casually as he watched the squad car drive off.

Lanie's temper flared up again. "Indecent exposure, my butt!"

"Precisely," Frank reminded her with a smug grin. "You're standing here in your undies, and they're half off."

"I have my shorts on!" Lanie yelled. "Almost." The shorts were still part way down, and they were too tight with the wet and soggy material to pull them up again without a struggle.

She gave up, pulled off the shorts revealing slinky bikini panties, and turned her attention to him. "If I'm guilty of indecent exposure, so are you!"

"But I'm not indecent in my jockeys, this is my own property." Frank didn't care if that made sense or not, he just wanted to get his two cents in.

It was the last straw for Lanie. She made a quick grab and got hold of his jockey shorts, ripping them as she pulled them down. "What jockeys?"

He tripped and fell, the shorts tangled down around his ankles. He reached out and grabbed her calf, pulling her down on top of him. She could feel his hard arousal beneath her.

He grabbed her hair tightly in both hands and pulled her face down to his, whispering against her lips. "Lanie love, do you really want to fight now?"

He raised up slightly, pressing his hardness into the juncture of her thighs and all the fight drained right out of her. Suddenly Frank didn't seem like such a bad guy after all.

"No." It was a soft, quiet admission, but she grinned as she asked, "Do you realize that you're laying out here in public, stark, staring naked? There must be someone close enough to see or hear us. After all, the cops were called."

"I am not stark staring naked!" he protested indignantly. "I'll have you know I still have my shoes and socks on."

Her anger had faded completely as her sense of humor took over. "I stand corrected, you are the very soul of decorum." She kissed the tip of his nose. "But let's go inside anyway."

"Better yet, let's go back to my old apartment. Remember, there's no water in this house because you had to have it turned off again." He kissed her back. "And we both need a shower."

"I really have to get home soon," Lanie told him reluctantly. "My watch has stopped. Frank, what time is it?"

"About 5:30," Frank told her.

"Oh no! I'm really late," Lanie said with concern. "My sitter's probably already mad."

"Grab your phone. I'll drive and you can call her on the way to my place, please." Frank was gently persistent. "Please, Lanie."

Lanie knew from the way he said the words "please, Lanie" that she was going to his place for much more than a shower. Her pulse raced and she began to smile, but she still hesitated for a moment, thinking.

She met his gaze squarely as she considered, and finally she said firmly, "Yes. I'll go to your apartment if I can get someone to watch Cassie."

"We're going to have to take your company jeep though, my car is mired too deep in the mud." He paused. "Can you do me a favor? My suitcases are in the trunk, could you please get my jogging shorts and sweat shirt out?" Frank laughed ruefully.

"Before those cops come back again and arrest me for indecent exposure this time."

Lanie looked him over but the mud provided more coverage than he realized. Darn! She thought lecherously. She stood up, pulled her shorts on quickly, and made her way carefully through the mud and retrieved his keys. Searching through the matching suitcases in his trunk, she found a pair of jogging shorts and a tank top. Grinning, she pulled off her soggy shorts with a great deal of wiggling, and put on Frank's clothes, pulling them right over her muddy underwear.

"Thanks Frank," she teased, "I was feeling a bit exposed out here in public wearing only my bra and panties."

"Lanie," he growled menacingly, "those are my clothes."

"And I borrowed them." She stuck her tongue out at him before turning back to the car and finding a navy blue fleece jogging suit that she held out to him. "Here, dear. Better cover up, it's getting cold and I wouldn't want anything important to freeze."

Frank looked around to make sure that no one was watching before he stood up and quickly pulled on the jogging pants and zipped up the matching jacket. Like Lanie, he pulled them on right over the mud that was sticking to his body. "Thanks."

"I'll drive," Frank said teasing her, "you know how bad a driver you are when you get distracted."

Surprisingly, she agreed, "If I'm not distracted now, I never will be. Let's put your suitcases and stuff into the back of the jeep."

They loaded Frank's luggage and got into her jeep, then she made the call to her sitter before Frank had even managed to get the jeep onto the street. As was expected, her sitter was already mad. She understood about the broken water pipe but she was really ticked off that Lanie hadn't called sooner. She had even tried to reach Tina to come take care of Cassie so that she could leave. Her own kids were already home from school and her husband was expecting his dinner.

After a short conversation, the sitter finally accepted Lanie's apology and her offer of an extra thirty dollars above the overtime she had coming, but with the stipulation that she could go home very soon.

Lanie glanced at Frank's face. Even though he only heard half of the conversation, he had heard enough to be clearly disappointed. She smiled at him reassuringly and placed a second call.

"Please be there, please be there, please be-" she whispered before the phone was picked up. "Tina, this is me, I need a favor. Can you please get over to my house and watch Cassie for me?" She listened for a while before she said, "I don't know." Her voice dropped and she continued, "With any luck, all night, if you can stay." She held the phone away from her ear as Tina let out a shriek. "Was that a yes?" She turned to Frank with a smile like a little girl on Christmas morning. "It was a yes."

"Thank God!" Frank's own smile was overjoyed.

The short drive from Frank's new house to his old apartment seemed to take forever, even though the drive was completed as fast as safety and the traffic law allowed. Frank found himself being distracted by Lanie's shy but eager smile. She had enough sense to avoid doing anything overtly distracting such as putting her hand on his thigh, but the looks she gave him and her restless anticipation were enough to drive him up the wall. Only sheer determination got them there safely. Frank and Lanie each grabbed some of his luggage out of the jeep, and then they made their way up to his apartment, suitcases in hand.

Chapter Thirteen

Once Frank and Lanie were actually inside his apartment, they each felt a small moment of hesitation, as though they both realized that the step they were about to take would dramatically change their relationship and possibly even their lives forever. This was certainly not a casual fling. No way!

Feeling almost stunned, Lanie watched as Frank let go of her hand and walked around the large apartment. He was almost wandering, not sure of his next move. That was totally unlike him. Although he was not a player, he was usually confident with women.

He had a way of putting his partners at ease with his natural charm, his genuine caring, and his sense of humor. Suddenly that charm and humor didn't seem to be enough because this was too important. He looked across the room and watched Lanie as she looked around at her surroundings.

The apartment was, she vaguely noticed, sleekly furnished with modern, expensive furniture. Black leather, glass, and chrome were all over the place, highlighted by several colorful paintings on the stark off-white walls. There was a bookshelf stocked with a wide variety of books, everything except romance novels, it seemed. Then she noticed a few Intimate Moments stacked on the corner of the middle shelf.

"You read romance novels?" She was surprised.

"Uh, someone must have left them there, maybe Kate or Laura. I read the first one out of curiosity and I liked it. I was surprised at how sensual it was," Frank admitted. "Now if Kate or Laura read one they think I might like, they bring it over after they've finished it. After all, I can't just go to the store and buy them as it would ruin my manly reputation."

She looked at him with a hint of mischief in her eyes. "Your secret's safe with me, Big Guy. Interesting decor, by the way, did you do it yourself?" she asked casually.

"Huh? Oh no, it was furnished this way when I moved in, except for the paintings," he said, distracted. "The place always seemed sort of cold and sterile to me until I put them up and added a bit of color."

"The pictures really do help," Lanie murmured as she walked across the room to Frank and once again took his hand. He brought her hand to his mouth and kissed the palm gently.

"Enough about my décor." Still holding Lanie's hand he asked, "Are you hungry? I can fix us something to eat or order a pizza while you take your shower, if you wish."

"Or you could shower first while I cook," Lanie retorted, grinning, "but that's not what I'd prefer."

"What would you prefer?" he asked cautiously.

"I'd prefer that we showered together and then ordered a pizza so that it would arrive after." She grinned in anticipation. "After we've finally made love for the first time, that is."

"Lanie, lady, I like the way you think." Frank hugged her and they made their way to the large bathroom. "I don't know why I got the idea you were so reticent."

"Yeah, you really read me wrong there," Lanie said firmly. "It's just that Cassie's father, the creep, made me suppress any wild impulses I had."

"You never have to suppress your impulses with me, Lanie love. Let yourself go." Frank's smile was wide, then he raised one eyebrow and said, "There's just one thing that bugs me, one tiny little problem."

"What's that?" she asked wide-eyed.

"I want my clothes back!" He tried to sound ferocious.

"Well, possession is nine-tenths of the law and I have them now. In fact as you can see I'm wearing them and I like it, so if you want to get them back you'll just have to take them right off me." Her defiance was playful.

Frank turned on the water in the shower bathtub combination stall and adjusted the water temperature before turning back to her with a fierce growl, "All right, I will."

He reached out quickly and pulled down his jogging shorts, sliding them down her shapely legs.

"I'll get you for that, you fiend." She reached out and unzipped the top half of his jogging suit.

Before she could slide the jogging top off of his broad shoulders however, he was working her tank top up over her head. She took her turn, working the jacket completely off of him. He responded by unfastening the front of her bra and dropping the muddy garment on the floor.

"Hey! That wasn't yours!" she protested. "That was my bra to begin with."

"If you can steal my clothes, I can steal yours," Frank countered.

"Yeah, but I can wear your clothes." She looked down at the bra and grinned. "Can you wear mine?"

"Good point," he managed to mumble.

She knelt down to pull his shoes and socks off as he balanced on first one foot and then the other. When she straightened up he very slowly slid her silky underwear down her legs until they fell to the floor, and then he lifted her gently out of the small pile of clothes jumbled up on the floor and set her in the shower under the warm spray. Quickly his jogging pants hit the floor and he joined her under the warm shower spray.

"I can't believe this is finally happening," Lanie murmured.

"Neither can I, my love." Frank kissed her quickly but deeply. "Now, stand still and let me wash this mud off that perfect skin. I want to see the woman underneath all that mud."

She was excited and dazed, but there was also an undercurrent of tension that was almost fear, a delicious sort of fear.

She hadn't been with many men in her life and she had been deeply hurt and wounded by Cal, her first real love. It had been years since she had let her guard down enough to get close to any man.

Now, here with Frank, she knew that if he hurt her the pain would be immeasurable, much worse than anything she had ever felt before. She trusted Frank not to hurt her intentionally but there were no guarantees. There was a time in every relationship, what a sterile word she thought to herself, when you had to open yourself up to possible pain.

Smiling to herself, she remembered Kate's question and answered it silently to herself: Yes, living without Frank was worse than her fear of what he could do to her. Definitely!

Frank began gently soaping her skin. She closed her eyes, savoring the feel of his hands roaming tenderly over her body, cleansing her of the sticky, partially dried mud and exploring her smooth skin and feminine contours. His hands also rinsed away the last of her nerves and doubts.

"You can't believe this is happening?" Frank teased, "You were the slow one. You were the one who held back, I've wanted to be with you like this forever."

"Frank, please understand, I had my reasons for waiting," she admitted softly. "It's been a long time."

"I know," he told her simply, "I understand, Lanie love."

He kissed her gently, exploring her mouth and seducing her with his tongue. She reached for the soap and began lathering his chest, running her thumbnails lightly over his nipples.

"Hey! Did you really say we'd waited forever?" She barely managed to whisper, "It just seems like we waited forever. Actually, we've known each other less than a month."

"In this case, that's forever. I wanted you from the first moment I saw your eyes shooting fire at me, and from your first words to me." He smiled at her, almost melting her bones.

"Which were as I recall, 'You great, big lumbering oaf!'

accompanied by a slap across your smug face," Lanie recollected.

"That's what did it, there's no accounting for taste," Frank shrugged as he stroked her firm breasts, "but now that I have you here, at last, I'm not going to rush anything, as much as I want to. I'm going to take this very slowly. I want to savor every second, every tenth of a second with you."

He took the soap away from her and lathered her breasts again, concentrating on her nipples, then he worked his way down her body, slowly and luxuriously. Her eyelids closed and her head tilted back as his magic fingers found her moist femininity. Her hands resting on his shoulders, he teased her there gently for a timeless moment, and then very deliberately, almost agonizingly, he moved on down her body. He knelt and washed her feet and legs.

"Turn around." It was a softly whispered command.

Still kneeling, he began to work his way slowly back up her body. She yelped as she felt a soft nip on her full, round bottom. His fingers and tongue gently explored every inch of her. She shivered as his fingers teased at her from behind, not really invading her core of moisture but tantalizing her. He stood and continued his task, slowly and maddeningly climbing up her body until she was totally limp. Finally, he picked up the shampoo and lathered her luscious fiery hair.

His hands felt delicious moving gently through her hair and massaging her scalp. As he stood close behind her, she could feel his manhood pressing against her. She stuck her head under the full force of the shower spray and rinsed, then he worked his fingers through her hair, making sure every trace of the shampoo was removed before he applied the conditioner. He rinsed all the conditioner out of her hair, and then she turned around again.

"Is it my turn now?" she asked, turning to face him, her voice soft and husky.

"Oh no, my love, not yet." He kissed her with love and passion.

Finally he left her mouth to chew on her neck, and then he moved on down her body. This time his hands and mouth followed the same path he had previously taken with the soap, down the front of her lovely body. He teased and suckled first one breast, then the other, his fingers teased and tormented her feminine core before his mouth followed. This time he didn't hurry on down to her toes. This time he lingered, loving her with hands and mouth until she screamed in delight, her fingers twisting in his hair, and shutters wracking her entire body.

"*Now* is it my turn?" Her voice sounded weak and thready as she asked the question. "I want to pleasure you, too."

"You are pleasuring me, love." Frank stood and kissed her, sharing the taste of her passion with her. "Just by being here with me and letting me love you."

"That's not what I meant." She sounded almost impatient.

"I know."

Ignoring the water still pelting down on his head, he managed to sit down and stretch his legs out in the bathtub. He reached both hands up and gently pulled her down into his lap.

"For now, my love," he cuddled her gently, kissing her hair, "just relax and let go. You'll get your turn later."

She did just that, kissing him lovingly and resting in his arms, feeling weak and spent, and very loved. As her breathing slowed and her heartbeat returned to normal, she began to tease him, her hands exploring his body. She slid them over his chest, teasing his taut nipples. Finally she lowered her hands, gently stroking his full erection. Somehow, with willpower he never knew he possessed, he stopped her before he'd had his full pleasure. Without a word, he handed her the shampoo and she washed his hair, then rinsed and conditioned it.

"Please, let me really love you," she protested again, whispering against his lips, "let me pleasure you."

"Oh my love, you do pleasure me." He kissed her. "More than you can possibly know, but let's get out of this shower first.

If you touch me any more, I may explode and I want our first time to be in a real bed."

"Good idea, if I can just get my feet under me." She smiled widely. "Besides, I'm beginning to look like a prune."

"Didn't I ever tell you?" Frank laughed, "I love prunes."

Somehow they managed to untangle their feet and stand up. Hand in hand, they climbed out of the bathtub and slowly, ever so slowly, dried each other off, both of them savoring the texture of the terry cloth against their skin.

The towels were discarded and they walked naked into his bedroom and over to his king-sized bed. The dim light from the bathroom gave the room an almost mystical glow. She stood there totally relaxed and unashamed in her nakedness, all of her fears and inhibitions completely gone. She watched him pull down the deep maroon velour bedspread and turn back the crisp white sheets. She took the time to fully appreciate watching the play of the muscles in his back and legs, and to study the firm, taut roundness of his buttocks. Her silent inspection was the continuation of the delightful survey that she had begun in the shower. He turned and held out a hand to her, and she hesitated just for a minute as she looked at his firm, well-muscled chest and his fully erect manhood.

"Nervous?" he asked gently, noticing her strange expression.

"No," she answered mischievously, "just enjoying the view."

She would have to find a way to show him that she wasn't the shy, nervous woman he thought she was. He was being so patient and careful with her and she appreciated it, but in a real relationship he would have to learn just how strong and deliciously wicked her sensual side could be.

Reaching out she took his hand and together they sank onto the bed. For a while they just laid there, side by side, barely touching each other. For a moment it was enough to be there together, drinking in the heady feeling of being with each other, almost wallowing in the anticipation of their lovemaking.

"Frank?" Lanie's voice was quiet in the dimly lit room.

"Yes, love," Frank answered softly.

"Love me now, please?" she begged. "You're taking too long."

"Yes love, I will." He moved over her, smiling down into her eyes, tenderly, and said, "I thought you'd never ask."

He lowered his mouth to hers and the magic began. They kissed forever, her hands exploring his broad chest and moving even lower. His hands teasing and tormenting her full breasts.

Frank said quietly, "Wait here." He turned on the bedside lamp. "I want to fulfill one of my fantasies about you."

He got out of the bed and headed back to the bathroom. He turned off the light and returned in just a moment with a plastic bottle of deliciously scented skin lotion.

"My sister left this here during her last visit." He grinned.

Working slowly and patiently he applied the lotion to her arms, all the way down to her fingertips. He went down to give the same treatment to her legs and feet. He returned to her chest, sliding and stroking the sensuous lotion on her chest and breasts and abdomen.

"Turn over," he ordered lovingly.

He slid the lotion all over her silky back and legs, working down to the tips of her toes. He rolled her over and began kissing her all over until she begged him to love her.

"Please love, come to me," she whispered in his ear, "I want to feel you inside me."

"Yes, Lanie love." He entered her in a hard, fast thrust, filling her completely. He nibbled her neck and gently sucked until a love bite appeared on her breast. Her long fingernails made scratches on his back.

He slowed his pace, gently stroking her as he slid in and out of her so slowly that she felt his body in exquisite detail, every millimeter. Finally, very slowly, his tempo increased. She met his sensuality completely.

They both instinctively knew what would give the other the greatest pleasure, each other's sensitive spots and special rhythms. It was a once in a lifetime match, with both sharing equally passionate natures, quirky senses of humor, and a certain wild sensuality.

She pulled him even closer, urging him on and meeting his powerful thrusts with her own frantic passion. Her heels rubbed the back of his thighs, and she was moaning and whispering frantically, "Come on."

He built a rhythm from slow and easy to fast and furious without ever letting either of them go over the edge. Time after time he pulled back just at the last instant, prolonging the waves of pleasure until finally they both went over the edge and flew into space in a perfect climax.

They lay there cuddled up together, not talking, spent and drained. Slowly as they both seemed to come out of the daze, they began to touch each other in little ways. Not to renew their passion, but just because they couldn't keep their hands off one another.

Gradually Lanie came out of her sensual fog and said, "Am I crazy or was that unbelievable?"

"Lady, we're dynamite together." Frank kissed her gently.

"I wonder if it'll be like that every time we make love," she mused aloud. "If it is, I've got to get hold of some vitamins, and fast."

"Don't worry, if we keep making love like that I don't think we'll live very long." Frank lay back on his pillow, exhausted and very happy.

"But what a way to go!" She climbed on top of him, wiggling as she settled onto him. "Hey lover, want to risk your life again?"

His exhaustion faded as he reached up to fondle her full breasts. "What the heck. My life insurance is all paid up."

Those were the last coherent words either one spoke for a very long time. This time after they made love, they drifted off to sleep in each other's arms. They even fit perfectly together in their sleep.

Lanie awoke before he did. She lay there in the faint, early morning light and thought of all he'd done to her, for her, and with her during the long night. She remembered her silent vow to show him, really show him, that she wasn't as shy and delicate as he seemed to think. Just because she'd backed off a few times when he had seemed to be getting to close. How could she prove it to him? She smiled to herself as she thought of the most wonderfully risqué way she could do it.

Frank awoke to the strange but delicious sensation of some-one stimulating and arousing him. Slowly, he became aware of several things: Lanie's mouth and hands roaming over his chest, teasing his nipples into tiny nubs with her tongue, and the soft sheets tied tightly around his wrists and fastened to the bedposts. Her tender, loving exploration continued on further down his body. She laved his navel before she went lower still. Realizing that he was fully awake and fully aroused, she looked up at him for just a moment.

"Well, you were greedy last night." She grinned. "You never gave me my turn to drive you wild, so I decided to take things into my own hands. You're not the only one with fantasies, you know." She lowered her mouth to him and drove him insane.

"I'm helpless and at your mercy." He smiled. "Do whatever you want with me. I promise I'll enjoy it."

"You bet your gorgeous behind you will." She grinned.

She spent a long time teasing and loving him. Then she really surprised him. She got off the bed and left him, totally ignoring his loud protests. It seemed like forever to Frank before she returned. When she did, in her hands she held a can of whipped cream.

She was shaking it with a devilish gleam in her eyes as she said, "It was fortunate for me that you had this in your refrigerator, wasn't it?"

He didn't have the words to answer but he was swallowing rapidly, his Adam's apple jumping in his throat.

She squirted the cool whipped cream on his body and her sweet, loving torture began anew.

All too soon she left him again, still tied to the bed. Once more, she went into the kitchen. He waited in sweet agony for her to return. The smell of coffee and bacon soon filled the air.

When she returned she started playing at his feet, working her way up his body. He was still hard and aching with desire. She continued teasing him without taking him over the edge for a long, long time.

Suddenly, instead of incoherent moans, he managed to speak up, stopping her. "I want to be inside you, Lanie love."

She brought her mouth up to his with a laugh and said, "Well, I guess that's okay with me if you insist."

She quickly untied him. He rolled over her and entered her in one smooth, hard thrust. It was a fast and furious lovemaking, with Frank's gentle restraint and control completely gone.

By the time his alarm clock went off, they were finished. It was time to get up but neither one of them could move an inch. They were exhausted. Their night, their incredible night was over, but the day held the promise of many fantastic nights to come.

"Wow!" he said, exhausted. "And to think, I thought you were a little inhibited."

"Not any more." She cuddled up to him. "You are the one responsible for bringing me out of my shell."

"I just didn't realize how far out of the shell you would come." He laughed.

"And I even made us breakfast." She grinned. "We may need to keep our strength up."

"Don't even say the word UP around me for a while, okay?" Frank moaned, teasing her.

"Then let's go eat that breakfast," she suggested, pulling him out of bed.

Chapter Fourteen

"I can take the day off work," Frank offered over breakfast. "I always get at least one day off after a business trip; besides, I'm not really due back until Monday. How about you?"

"Are you nuts?" Lanie laughed. "Landscaping your house is my biggest job right now and we have to fix the pipe and let your property dry off before we can do any more. Besides, Jack is one of my partners, and Laura would kill him if he didn't cover for me today."

"Then I propose that we take a short nap, make love again, then shower, and after that take Cassie out to do something fun for the day." He kissed her. "I have the strangest feeling I should get to know her better, real soon. I just hope she likes me."

"She liked you a lot when she went to the hospital after she cut her face. She kept telling me how nice you were. She'll like you." Lanie smiled at him and continued, "She's got great taste, besides she can be bribed. I can think of several things she'd like, not that I would suggest you try to buy her affection, of course."

"Of course not," Frank said as they left the table. "But as long as I'm not buying her affection, what would she want?"

"I think the best thing you can give her is a fun day." She kissed him. "Maybe the beach," another kiss, "maybe Disney-land," another kiss, "maybe horseback riding, she loves horses." A long deep kiss. "But that's after you give me what I want, and I want you deep inside me right after I make a quick phone call." She reached for the bedside phone.

Lanie called home. "How is everything?"

140

"Cassie is getting ready for school. I was just about to take her," Tina replied. "As it is, I called in and said I'd be late for work."

"I'll call the school and tell them Cassie's sick because the three of us are going to spend the day together," Lanie said. "Frank wants to get to know her. We'll come home and get her in a little while. Will you be able to stay until we get there?"

"No problem, they just put me down for the night shift. So? How was the night?" Tina had held the question back as long as she could.

"The words to describe last night don't exist, not in this world. Tina, you've got to let Kate and Laura go to work on you." Lanie laughed. "I thought I was happy as a single mom, I really did. Now I know what I've been missing. I'm stunned."

"I'm so happy for you," Tina told her. "No one deserves that kind of happiness more than you."

Lanie hung up the phone and looked at Frank. "I need you, Frank." She reached for him and led him back to the bedroom.

"I aim to please." Frank poised himself over her.

"And you've got darn good aim." She wrapped her arms around him and once again they left the world far behind.

In the end it was the pleasant morning-after lassitude that determined how Frank and Lanie would spend the day with Cassie. To put it simply, Frank and Lanie were both way too tired to spend the day walking around Disneyland, and Lanie's legs were a bit too stiff to really enjoy horseback riding. That left the beach. Besides that, it was a perfect southern California beach day, sunny and hot.

Just a few minutes after they made love again, Lanie dragged herself out of bed and into the shower. This time, at her insistence, she showered alone. Frank pretended to be put out but he knew exactly why she wanted to shower by herself. He realized that if he joined her in the shower, they'd never get over to Lanie's house to pick Cassie up. While Lanie was still in the shower the phone rang.

Frank paced over to the phone and answered it. "Hello."

It was Kate calling from the office. She said, "Welcome back to civilization, Frank. How was your trip?"

"It was okay," Frank said noncommittally, "just a few days too long. I missed Lanie."

"I know, she missed you, too." Kate smiled as she leaned back in her office chair. "Congratulations on the promotion, Frank, you really deserved it. I hope you had a good time in Texas, but Bob said you probably didn't because corporate headquarters can be fairly stuffy and boring. By the way, I left something special for you and Lanie outside your apartment door. I hope you both enjoy it. Oh, by the way, tell Lanie I said good-morning and give her a kiss for me."

"I will when I see her," Frank said vaguely.

"Which will be in about five minutes when she gets out of the shower," she stated with authority.

"Why do you think she's here?" Frank wondered.

Kate didn't reply, she just gave a kind of snort and hung up with a decisive click.

Frank replaced the receiver as soon as he heard the click. Lanie came out of the shower drying herself and looking at Frank with a question in her eyes. Ignoring her questioning glance, he strode to the apartment door and opened it. Outside he found a wicker picnic basket, a red and white plastic cooler, a beach blanket, and a large plastic shopping bag. He brought everything inside the apartment.

"What's that?" Lanie asked curiously.

"A care package from Kate," he told her, examining the picnic basket. "She really should work for one of those psychic networks. She knew we'd spend the day together, and I think she knew just how we plan to spend it. She packed everything we need for a day at the beach."

"Does she know we spent the night together?" Lanie

wondered.

"Yes, but I'm not sure how she knew it. She did say to tell you good morning when you got out of the shower," Frank gave her a mind-numbing kiss, "and to give you a wake-up kiss."

"That kiss felt like it was entirely your idea," Lanie whispered breathlessly. She raised up on her toes for another kiss, her lips lingering against his mouth. "What's in the bag?"

"Check it out." Handing her the bag he said, "I've found a note." He read the note to himself.

"She's bought some clothes for me. Black shorts and a white T-shirt, plus there's a tiny green print bikini far too revealing for me to actually wear out in public, and a wrap around skirt in a matching fabric, sunscreen, and a new toothbrush," Lanie inventoried the bag. "Everything's even the right size."

"Lanie, just this once, wear the bikini." Frank leveled a gaze at her. "For me?"

"I'll think about it." Frank's gaze made her feel warm all over.

"Listen to this: 'I figured you two would want to spend the day together with Cassie. I'd suggest a lazy day at the beach or even a private day by our pool. I put a set of our house keys in the picnic basket for you. Bob and I are going to take the kids to a movie after work so we won't get home until after seven. P.S. I hope you like chocolate mousse and strawberries.'" Frank put down the note. "Well, now that you have clothes, get dressed! Let's go!"

Lanie pulled on the bikini and put the shorts and T-shirt over it. Frank showered quickly and got dressed in his black swimming trunks and a soft blue T-shirt. He put the picnic basket, blanket, and the cooler in the jeep.

"Frank, we need to drop this jeep off at the company yard and pick up my car." Lanie directed him to where her own car was parked, and once there, they transferred the cooler and picnic basket to the trunk of her car. Then they went to Lanie's house and picked up Cassie.

As soon as Lanie's car pulled up in front of the house, Cassie came bounding out of the house in her red and white swimsuit. She had a towel, a pair of shorts and a t-shirt in a bag.

"Hi Mom! Hi Frank! Boy! This is going to be neat!" Cassie exclaimed. "I get to spend a day at the beach instead of going to school."

She accepted a hug from Lanie before she settled in the backseat and fastened her seatbelt without any prompting. She was excited and exhilarated. Her mood was catching, Lanie and Frank exchanged wide grins as they buckled up before they started the car and drove away.

"I'm glad you like the idea, Cassie," Frank said as soon as he started the car. "I really wanted to spend some time with you and get to know you better. I'm glad you remember me. I see your face has healed really well, I can hardly see where you cut it."

"I know, I remember you were at the hospital. I also remember talking to you at that funny wedding with the puppies." Like a typical kid, out of all that happened that day the puppies stood out the clearest in her mind. Remembering them, she giggled before continuing, "I also read some of the notes you sent to my Mommy as her secret admirer. They were pretty neat, but some of them were kinda silly. I liked the presents."

"I didn't write all the notes, so I don't know if I wrote the silly ones and the only presents I sent her were the pearls. Somebody else must have sent the other presents," Frank shrugged, "but anyway, your Mommy's really special and I like her a whole lot." Frank smiled into the rearview mirror. "I hope we can be friends, too."

"So far, so good," the precocious nine-year-old said, grinning.

Frank laughed, amused and surprised by the girl's spirit. He thought to himself about how much she took after her mother. It was just a short ride to the beach and since school was in session, there wasn't the usual fruitless search for a decent parking space. Sometimes you had to trail people as they walked towards a car hoping to get their space as they left. They didn't have that problem. In fact, it seemed like only minutes until they were spreading out the blanket in a prime spot not too far from a lifeguard tower.

The sand was warm and perfect, and they were just far enough from the lapping waves so they could stay several hours before the tide would move them farther back up the beach. Lanie almost immediately shed her outer clothes and laid out on the big beach blanket. Frank wound up with sunscreen duty, gently applying it to Lanie's back, and then to Cassie's. Lanie returned the favor and spread some on his back, before she settled back on the blanket and shut her eyes.

"Frank, do you want to take a walk with me?" Cassie asked eagerly.

"How about your mom?" Frank asked.

"She can come too, of course, but she looks kinda tired to me. What did you two do all night?" Cassie asked, innocently.

"Cassie!" Lanie interrupted, blushing. She sat up again and said, "Let me put some sunscreen on you before you and Frank go wandering off."

"Frank already did, Mommy, remember?" Cassie said, sounding a bit irritated. "I just wanted to find out if you and Frank had a good time last night."

Frank smothered a grin as he knelt down on the blanket. "Yeah, Lanie, did you and I have a good time last night?"

"You know we did." Lanie's smile was age-old, knowing and mysterious at the same time.

"Frank, will you tell me what you and Mommy did?" Cassie turned to him. "She's so tired."

"What did your Mommy and I do last night?" He sent Lanie a look that caused shivers to run down her spine. "Well, your Mommy was really muddy, so I made sure she took a long shower then we had a really good dinner, and we talked and listened to music all night long. Will you spread some lotion on my chest, too?"

"Only if you promise to return the favor." Lanie smiled, rubbing the cool lotion on Frank's broad chest.

"My pleasure, Ma'am." The smile was devilish. He took the lotion and very gingerly rubbed Lanie's shoulders and her chest above the bikini top.

"What else did you two do?" Cassie probed. "She's too tired for just talking. Did you kiss her?"

"Well," Frank drew out the word, "yeah, a few times. Girls like that, you know. Grown up girls."

"What else?" Cassie insisted.

"Well, I tickled her and we wrestled with each other a little bit," Frank admitted. "Of course, we stayed up very late."

"It sounds like it was fun." Cassie decided, "I wish I'd been there with you." She and Frank walked off hand in hand while Lanie stretched out again on the blanket.

Cassie's curiosity wasn't satisfied for long, however, and as soon as they were out of earshot from Lanie she looked up at Frank with another question burning in her eyes.

Finally she asked, "Are you going to be my Daddy?"

"I'm not sure." Frank had enough experience with kids to answer as honestly as possible. "I think it's a good possibility, but it's too soon to be sure. You're a big part of the decision, you know. I love your mother, but we haven't known each other very long. Of course, you have to be part of the family, a very important part of the family, so you and I have to get along, too."

"I think we will." Cassie met his gaze with her little chin up and said, "As long as you're nice to my Mommy and to me." The imp grinned. "A day off from school now and then and an ice cream sundae once in a while wouldn't hurt either."

"A day off from school is a rare treat, and only for a girl who is getting very good grades," Frank said sternly before he grinned. "Ice cream, however, is a necessity of life."

"Do you have any pets?" Cassie asked hopefully.

"No, why?" Frank asked with curiosity.

"I was just hoping you had a dog," she told him. "I've always wanted one but I've never had one."

"I live in an apartment, so there's no room for a dog to run and play," he told her. "But I'm moving into a house soon, a big house with as large yard, so I expect I'll get a puppy soon."

"Can I play with it?" she asked with a wistful tone in her voice.

"Of course you can, Sweetie." Frank leaned down to hug her. "A puppy needs all the love it can get."

"Neat." Cassie grinned, melting his heart.

Frank took Cassie over to the lifeguard tower and introduced her to the lifeguard before he picked up the little girl and carried her out into the ocean. He held her high in the air, causing her to shrill with delight before dropping her into the cool shallow water. Soon they were in a major water fight accompanied by girlish squeals, masculine shouts, and lots of splashing. When they walked back to the beach blanket they noticed that Lanie was still sound asleep.

"Let's build a sandcastle and let your Mommy sleep," Frank suggested. "She must really need it."

"Great!" Cassie grabbed her plastic bucket and pail. "Frank? Did you enjoy the mystery train trip? My grandma said you would."

Frank was already digging in the sand like an overgrown child. He paused and looked up at her. "What?"

"Did you like the trip?" she repeated. "On the train."

Frank answered, "It was great! We had a lot of fun and really got to spend some time together. Did your grandma send the tickets?"

"She bought the tickets but I thought it up," Cassie said proudly. "I heard my friend say that her parents went on a trip like that and they liked it. I thought you and Mommy would enjoy it."

"You're too smart for your own good, Cassie." Frank was stunned, realizing that he'd just discovered the final secret admirer. "But let's see if you can build a castle."

Together they built a truly sad, lop-sided, but somehow grand sandcastle. They dug a moat to keep most of the rising tide from ruining their masterpiece too soon. Finally, Cassie complained that she was getting hungry. They walked hand in hand back to the blanket where Lanie slept.

"Lanie, wake up!" Frank told her. "We're hungry."

"How long have I been asleep?" Lanie shrugged herself awake.

"A couple of hours. We've been swimming, had a real water fight, and we built a really neat sandcastle. Lop-sided and all, it was perfect." He sat down on the blanket beside her and continued, "But now we're hungry."

"Mommy?" Cassie asked. "Am I still going to my Girl Scout meeting this afternoon?"

"Would you like to?" Lanie asked.

"Well, they're planning our campout, and the leader told us we should be sure to come to this meeting if we want to go," Cassie explained. "I really want to go to the campout."

"Then you should go to the meeting. After we eat lunch we'll take you to it, okay?" Lanie told her.

They opened the picnic hamper and got out the plastic utensils, paper plates and cups. They also found biscuits and jelly in the hamper. They dug into the cooler and feasted on the lunch of cold fried chicken, potato salad, and coleslaw. They also found a large bottle of soda in the cooler, along with some bottled water. There was also a special dessert in the hamper: chocolate cupcakes with tiny sprinkles on top.

As soon as they finished the lunch they packed up their stuff. They took another walk along the beach, this time resulting in a three-way water fight.

Finally, Lanie tied on her wraparound skirt and both she and Frank put on their t-shirts. Even Cassie had some clean shorts and a t-shirt she'd brought along. They drove Cassie to her Girl Scout meeting at the troop leader's house.

As Cassie got out of the car she said, "Thanks Frank. I had a super day. I think you'd make a great daddy." She hugged him quickly.

Frank was clearly taken aback but he recovered quickly and said, "Thank you Cassie, I think that's the nicest thing anyone has ever said to me."

"Will I see you again?" she asked earnestly.

"Real soon, Sweetie, real soon." He was clearly touched by Cassie's complete acceptance.

Cassie ran up the steps to the meeting with more energy that should be legal. Lanie trudged up the steps behind her and asked the troop leader if she could use her phone. She called Kate.

"Kate? This is Lanie," she said simply. "I need a favor."

"What can I do?" Kate's reply was instant and without hesitation.

"Could you pick Cassie up at her scout meeting and keep her with you and your kids until you get home?" Lanie asked. "Normally I'd ask Tina but she has the night shift tonight."

"No problem," Kate said cheerfully, "we'll enjoy it. Just give me the address and make sure the troop leader knows about it."

Lanie made the arrangements with the scout leader to have Kate pick up her daughter after the meeting and went back join to Frank in her car.

As soon as she got back to the car Lanie muttered, "She's a cute kid and I love her a whole lot, but I may have to strangle her real soon. How could she have embarrassed me that way? How could she have done that?"

"Done what?" Frank grinned and raised his brows questioningly. "She was perfectly behaved all day."

"She practically proposed to you," Lanie fumed, "telling you that you'd make a great Daddy."

"She's right. I'm gonna make a great daddy." Frank leaned over and kissed a shocked Lanie. "You just don't know it yet. Maybe your daughter is smarter than you are. Did you ever think of that? Let's go over to Kate and Bob's where we can play some adult games in private."

"Smarter than me?" Lanie was very quiet then said, "Or just easier to win over? After all, my affections can't be bought with a day at the beach or ice cream, I want more."

"Then I'll have to see that you get what you want, too." Frank leaned over and kissed her, his lips warm and lingering against her mouth. "For the rest of your life, if I can manage it."

"It's hard to argue with that." Lanie kissed him back.

He started the car. After a quick stop at the nearest store, they went over to Kate's house and found a note for them on the door. It read:

I knew you'd wind up here so there's a special treat for you in the refrigerator. For your information, our fences are high enough to allow you to swim in the nude, and the double wide inflatable mattress is perfect for making love on. We won't be home until seven, I guarantee it.
Have fun,
Kate.

Chapter Fifteen

When Frank and Lanie first entered Kate's house they were greeted by a bouncing Boston Terrier. He jumped all over, wiggling the stump of his almost non-existent tail and licking any piece of human skin he could reach with his long, agile tongue.

"Hiya Charger, how's my friend?" Frank picked up and cuddled the excited little dog. The dog wiggled so hard Frank had trouble holding onto him as he licked Frank's hands and face. "Hey! Knock it off, my face is clean! Lanie, meet Charger. He has a wife and two daughters around here somewhere."

"I saw him at the wedding with the Best Man." Lanie stroked Charger's sleek, round head. "I thought there were four puppies."

"Two have already gone to new homes," Frank said.

No sooner had the words left his mouth then a smaller version of Charger came wiggling up to them. She was a female puppy around two months old. Along with her was an older female Boston, obviously the puppy's mother. Another puppy followed not too far behind. Frank scooped the first puppy up and handed her to Lanie.

"This is Jojo. She's the real power in this household. She rules the roost." Jojo did her best to shower Lanie with affection. Frank put down Charger and picked up Oreo, hugging the squirming puppy. "And that's Teddy, her mom, and this is Oreo, her sister. Kate's keeping Jojo but Oreo needs a good home. I'm tempted to take her myself but I'm still thinking it over." He bent over to pet Teddy who immediately rolled over onto her back, positively begging to have her tummy rubbed. "To bad you weren't here a couple of weeks ago when Jojo and Oreo still had their sister and brother. It was a zoo with all four puppies running around."

"I'll bet." Lanie laughed as she got a puppy kiss. "They sure were a hit at the wedding, and they were great for the kids to play with. I'm surprised they weren't already sold."

"Kate thought she had Oreo sold, but the woman who was getting her decided to wait for Teddy's next litter because she decided a new puppy and a new baby were too much to handle all at once." Frank cuddled the wiggling puppy. "Her baby was born almost exactly two weeks before the puppies were ready to go to their new homes."

"That would be a lot to handle all at once," Lanie smiled at the thought of having a baby and a puppy, "but it would be a joy, too."

Leaving the dogs, who trailed behind them, he took Lanie's hand and led her into the kitchen. They found a note on the refrigerator door telling them to look inside. They found their treats on a tray inside the refrigerator. The tray had two bowls of chocolate mousse on it, both topped with a touch of whipped cream, shaved chocolate, and a cherry. There was also a bottle of champagne with their names on a note around the bottle's neck and a bowl of luscious, perfect strawberries, along with a can of whipped cream, and a couple of bottles of cola.

Seeing the can of whipped cream, Lanie blushed remembering her uninhibited and slightly risqué actions the last time she'd had her hands on the delightful topping. Whatever had possessed her to do such a thing? She had never acted like that before. It had been exquisite and decadent fun. Was it really just that morning?

Leaving the champagne, whipped cream, and strawberries, Lanie carried the rest of the treasures out onto the poolside deck. They sat side by side in the afternoon sun and ate their chocolate mousse and sipped their colas from tall glasses full of ice. The dogs watched them intensely as they ate but otherwise were well mannered. Finally the silent stares from big brown eyes got to Frank and he gave each dog a small taste of his mousse.

When they finished the desserts, Lanie carried them into the house and rinsed the dishes. She refilled the glasses with ice water and went out to join Frank on a chaise lounge.

"Leave it to Kate to have lounge chairs big enough for two," Frank noted, cuddling her in his arms.

"A woman after my own heart," Lanie agreed.

They lay there side by side, sipping their water and talking. Soon they added cuddling and exchanging gentle kisses. They stayed that way for a while but it was still hot and the pool looked so refreshing.

"Let's go for a swim," Lanie suggested, pulling off her skirt and grabbing her glass of water.

She opened the gate that completely surrounded the pool area and carefully shut it again leaving the dogs out. She sat her water down beside the pool and jumped into the warm pool. She floated and splashed around for a while before swimming a few fast laps with a strong, efficient stroke.

Frank watched for a while before he pulled off his T-shirt and joined her in the pool. He swam for a while before catching Lanie by her heels and pulling her over to him. He kissed her long and passionately until they both started to sink. Floating to the surface, Lanie breathed in a gulp of air and then grabbed Frank and returned the kiss, her hands sliding around his waist. Without warning, she pulled his swimming trunks down and let them float away.

"I wish you'd stop being so shy about letting me know what you want. Just come on and let me know," Frank quipped, treading water. "So you want to play dirty, little girl?"

"That's exactly what I want." Treading water, she reached behind her neck and unfastened the knot at the neck of her bikini top. "I knew you'd figure it out."

Frank swam around behind her and untied the thin strings

that ran across her back. Her top drifted away. From behind her, he stroked and fondled her breasts before he slowly reached down and pealed off her bikini bottom. He nibbled her neck and spread tender kisses on down her back to her round, firm rump.

Suddenly he dove under the water's surface and swam under her, turning over and sliding his body slowly up to the surface between her legs. Surfacing, he met her mouth in a frenzied kiss, his hands pulling her legs up to wrap around his waist, his tongue plunging deeply into her mouth as he entered her in a smooth strong thrust.

Frank soon realized that treading water and making love were not necessarily two activities that worked well together, so he worked his way to the shallow end. Bracing his legs, he slid slowly, languidly in and out of Lanie's tight, warm body. He reveled in the soft whimpering sounds she made in her throat. He used his hands, gripping Lanie's firm rounded buttocks to guide the action. As he raced towards a hard, fast climax he blocked out the outside world and all of its distractions. Lanie moaned and whimpered with the approach of her climax, finally screaming out in release.

Breathing heavily, Frank backed up to the side of the pool before he made his way to the steps, still holding Lanie in his arms. He sat down with Lanie in his lap, stroking her hair and placing little kisses all over her face.

They sat there on the pool steps for a long time before he got out and grabbed the big air mattress. He threw it into the pool and jumped in after it. He pushed it over to Lanie and held it steady while she got on. In turn, she used the side of the pool to hold it steady while he joined her on the large mattress. They floated and held each other. Gentle kisses were exchanged, lips meeting lips with more affection than passion.

Scooping at the water to maneuver the float over to the side of the pool, Lanie grabbed her water and took a long swallow. She offered some to Frank but he preferred to drink the coldness off her luscious lips. She barely managed to set the water glass down before he caught her mouth in a kiss that quickly moved from affection to full blown passion.

With a soft moan she opened to him fully, her mouth as his tongue sought hers, and her legs as he nestled between her strong, velvet thighs. Even her emotions and feelings opened to him fully. He shared all that he was with her and she took it, giving him her essence, her passion in return. They were lucky not to sink the mattress.

Afterwards, it took a long time for either to recover enough to breathe evenly, much less speak coherently. Eventually they began to talk softly and stroke each other. They were gentle strokes and touches not born of desire, but stemming from tender devotion.

"Lanie, when will you marry me?" The question was out before he had even thought about it. He kissed her deeply. "Cassie's already given me her approval."

Lanie gazed up at him, shocked and speechless. A fierce joy filled her. Subconsciously she realized she had expected his proposal eventually, but this seemed so sudden, so quick, and she admitted to herself, so right.

"Lanie love, are you all right?" Frank asked finally.

"I'm shocked, stunned, and speechless," she stopped and smiled, "and full of alliteration, it seems."

"Well, I proposed." Frank sounded almost stern. "What do you have to say about it?"

"You call that a proposal?" Lanie was stalling for time to sort out her feelings. "Whatever happened to a romantic setting? Passionate words of love? Getting down on one knee?"

"Going down on one knee? Lanie love, we're in the swimming pool, I'd drown!" Frank laughed then he sobered and said, "I'll admit it was a spur of the moment proposal and not the passionate and loving declaration that you deserve, but the meaning is the same: I do love you. You are the one I want to build my life with, to fight with and make love with, even just to sit beside when I watch old movies on television. Are you going to make us both happy and agree to marry me or follow your stubborn instincts and go down fighting?" he prodded.

"I think I'll give in now, make us both happy, and save my stubborn fighting instincts for later." She smiled at him, watching for his reaction. "I'm sure I'll need them sooner or later."

It was Frank's turn to be shocked and filled with sudden delight. He sat quietly for a minute before he gave a loud shout of pure joy and hugged her until she squealed and rolled them both off the mattress and into the water. They lay on the deck in the late afternoon sun and kissed and cuddled for a few minutes before Frank went in and brought out the champagne and strawberries.

"Kate really must be psychic." Frank grinned. "Knowing her, she already has an engagement ring picked out."

"She's not totally psychic," Lanie reminded him, "she didn't even know about her own wedding."

"That's true, but maybe her powers don't work on herself," Frank suggested. "Who cares? We have better things to do."

He picked up the full bottle and poured some of the cold champagne on her warm, still moist navel. He lowered his mouth to her and began drinking the liquid from her body before his lips and tongue went lower still. Soon, they had celebrated their engagement with the champagne and strawberries, and tender but passionate lovemaking.

"I should have brought out the whipped cream," Frank quipped, "since this morning you didn't let me have any at all."

The idyllic afternoon finally came to an end. They picked up everything around the pool and washed the dessert dishes quickly in Kate's immaculate kitchen, which gave the champagne time to wear off before Frank took Lanie home.

They made a stop on the way home to pick up some groceries, steaks and potatoes for dinner. Before dinner was ready

Lanie got a call from Kate asking if Cassie could stay with them overnight. She told Lanie that Cassie had already eaten her dinner.

"Don't worry about coming over to get her in the morning, either," Kate said, "I'll bring her over or call Tina to come get her. That way you can sleep in."

"Thanks, Kate." Lanie hung up.

"I'm a bad Mom," Lanie said with a grin, "I'm glad she won't be home until tomorrow if it gives me tonight with you."

"Oh?" Frank teased, "What do you want to do? There's a football game on TV."

"You're watching football tonight over my dead body." Lanie's eyes narrowed.

"Well, that's one way to watch football," Frank pondered, "but not my first choice."

"Let's fix dinner," Lanie said enigmatically, "then perhaps I can show you some other options."

"I like the way you think." Frank went outside and started the barbecue grill while Lanie fixed salads and put the potatoes into the microwave.

He threw on the steaks while she heated some sourdough bread rolls and also made iced tea. They sat down together at the kitchen table, ate their dinner, and talked about the future they planned to have.

"Do you think Cassie will really be happy if we get married?" Frank asked for the third time.

"I'm sure she will," Lanie said patiently, "she really likes you."

"It takes more than liking someone to think they'd make a good father," Frank pointed out, sipping his iced tea. "Some kids resent a stepfather."

"But those kids usually had a real father who they loved and didn't want to let go of. They sometimes feel that if they give the stepfather a chance, they're being disloyal to their real father. Also, sometimes the stepfather suffers in comparison to the real father," Lanie explained gently. "Cassie has no real father to be loyal to or to compare you with. She likes you already; in fact I think she already loves you."

"I sure love her," Frank admitted. "She stole my heart the second I met her."

"If she doesn't love you already, she will," Lanie teased, "after all, I was the one who was hard to convince."

They finished their dinner, washed dishes, and sat in front of the TV like a respectable married couple. Until bedtime, that is, when they went upstairs and tore the sheets up in their frenzied way.

The next morning reality set in as Cassie came home before they got out of bed.

"Oh my goodness!" Lanie woke up as soon as she heard the front door. She jumped out of bed and threw on her robe, something she almost never wore, and ran down the stairs to intercept her daughter and sister.

"I'm so glad you're home!" she told them brightly. "I'm just relaxing this morning, after all, it's Saturday. Tina, your car is blocking the driveway so you'll be the one who goes."

"Goes where?" Tina asked puzzled. "And why?"

"I want donuts," Lanie explained, trying to give Tina a meaningful look, "I just woke up this morning wanting donuts and you know what that means--I won't rest until I have some." She got out her wallet and handed Tina some money. "I'll even pay for them. Cassie, go with your Aunt Tina so that you can pick out the ones you like best."

"Aunt Tina knows what my favorites are," Cassie said, sounding faintly defiant. "I want to watch TV, the cartoons are on."

Tina caught on quickly and said, "Come on Cassie, you won't miss much and I really can use your help." She held out her hand to the girl. She heard a noise, faint but distinct from upstairs and cocked her head, a wide grin on her face. "I think you've got squirrels in the roof."

"Thanks, Tina," Lanie ignored the squirrel remark and put her wallet back in her purse, "I really appreciate this."

"I don't suppose you know what kind of donuts Frank likes?" Tina wondered. "I'm sure he'll be here by the time I get back."

"Just get out and get an assortment of donuts." Lanie pushed her sister out the door.

Frank came downstairs as soon as Tina and Cassie were gone. "I'm sorry, Lanie, I should have been up and gone before they got home."

"Nonsense," she kissed him quickly, "but it would have been nice if you had been up and dressed. If we both had been up and dressed."

"Did they know?" Frank asked, following her as she walked into the kitchen to make coffee.

"Tina did," Lanie started the coffee maker, "I doubt if Cassie realized anything." She turned to face him. "Are we going to tell them about us, that we're engaged?"

"I want to." Frank's answer was instant, his smile genuine. "I want to shout it from the rooftop. What about you?"

"Me too," she said, meeting his eyes, "but there is one thing, no two things we have to consider."

"Which are?" he asked gently.

"I told Cassie, in fact, we both told Cassie that it would be partly her decision if we got married," Lanie pointed out.

"So? We have to let her give her opinion and try to get her approval." Frank remembered promising the little girl that she would indeed factor into the decision. "What's the other thing?"

"My mother," Lanie said quickly. "She doesn't know a thing about you, and I think she should meet you and get to know you before we announce our wedding."

"She knows about me," Frank said calmly.

"What?" Lanie was puzzled. "How do you know that she knows?"

"She and Cassie were one of the secret admirers." Frank beamed at her. "They sent the tickets to the Mystery Train."

"How do you know?" Lanie was surprised.

"Cassie let it slip when we were building the sand castle yesterday." Frank remembered, "She said that her grandma said you and I would like the trip on the Mystery Train."

"So that's who the seventh secret admirer was." The last piece of the puzzle fell into place just as she heard Tina drive up. "So, what do we do?"

"How about if we ask Cassie and tell Tina," Frank suggested, "and ask them both to keep it a secret until we can tell your mother. Where does your mother live anyway?"

"My mother lives in Pasadena, not far from Santa Anita Racetrack," Lanie told him.

"She's not very old is she?" Frank said, "I couldn't have *The Little Old Lady From Pasadena* for a mother-in-law, it would be too weird."

"She's only twenty years older than I am, and she likes horse racing, not drag racing. But back to the matter at hand, a secret? Those two?" Lanie's voice reflected her disbelief. "Surely you jest."

"Yes, a secret," Frank deadpanned, "and don't call me Shirley. Why don't we call your mother and take her out to dinner tonight? Even those two can keep a secret that long."

"That sounds good." She moved into his arms and brought her mouth up for a kiss.

"Hi Frank," Cassie's voice brought them both back to reality, "I didn't know you'd be here."

"Hi Cassie. Hi Tina." Frank hugged the girl gently and asked, "What have you got there? It smells like donuts."

"It should. It *is* donuts." Tina greeted Frank.

Lanie poured some milk for Cassie and coffee for everyone else and they all sat at the kitchen table. She carefully selected her donut before she spoke. "Frank and I have something to discuss with both of you."

"Please say you're getting married. Please," Cassie said, looking at both of them in turn.

Frank met Lanie's eyes across the table. Her eyes were definitely moist with unshed tears and he realized his own were the same. "Yes Cassie, we are, if it's okay with you."

"Boy! Is it okay with me!" Cassie jumped out of her chair.

The room erupted with squeals and excited hugs of congratulations.

Chapter Sixteen

That evening the four of them, Frank, Lanie, Cassie, and Tina, drove up to Pasadena and took Lanie's mother, Jean, out to dinner to tell her the news. She intrigued Frank because she gave him a good idea about how Lanie would look in twenty years. She was a miniature version of Lanie but with some streaks of gray in her hair. She also had one feature in common with Tina, her freckles.

Jean was thrilled to meet Frank. She had heard great things about him from Cassie and also from Tina, so she was already prepared to like him. She was surprised, however, at just how much she liked him. It was not just his looks but she liked *him*, the man inside the face and the body. She was in heaven.

She had long since given up on either of her daughters finding a great husband. She didn't want them to settle for anyone even slightly less than the perfect catch, but lately, as long as the man was steady, reliable, and would treat her daughters right, she would have tried to accept anyone. With Frank, she didn't have to pretend to accept someone less than she thought Lanie deserved. Frank was far ahead of her wildest expectations. She decided he was almost too good to be true: handsome, well-spoken, good job, genuinely caring and full of kindness with Cassie, topped with a great sense of humor.

Jean had her own surprise for the four of them. She had accepted a new job and was moving to Arizona. "I wasn't sure if I wanted to take the job and move so far away from you but it's an excellent opportunity."

She taught botany at Pasadena City College; her new offer

was for a teaching position at Arizona State. In fact, she had already resigned from the City College and was starting at ASU for the fall semester.

"Mom, I'm so proud of you." Lanie hugged her mother. "Your love of botany gave me my love of landscaping."

"Well, before I go I do have one thing to do," she glanced over at Tina, "I have to talk to Kate and Laura about Tina."

"Gee, thanks Mom," Tina drawled, "don't go to any trouble on my account."

"Well, I would like to see you settled down before I move to Arizona, which will be in about a month," Jean told her.

"Mom, why haven't you told us about this move before?" Lanie asked.

To her surprise, her mother blushed before she answered, "When I heard the job was open, I applied for it. I didn't expect to be offered the job but I thought it might be a good bargaining tool when my raise and promotion came up. During the interview with the ASU department head something weird happened, it felt as if we'd known each other forever. I felt so comfortable with him. When the job was offered to me, I took it."

"You have a thing for your new department head?" Lanie yelped. "Is that wise?"

"Probably not," Jean admitted blushing, "but there it is."

"Did Kate or Laura have anything to do with you finding out about this opening?" Frank asked suspiciously.

"I don't know them except from what Cassie and Tina have told me," Jean said. "Why would they set me up?"

"Stranger things have happened," Lanie said dryly. "Why are you moving so soon? The next semester doesn't start for a couple of months. Heck, school's not even out yet."

"I need to settle in and get to know my way around the campus and the town," Jean told her, "and plan my courses."

"Well, we can celebrate your job and Lanie's engagement at

the same time, let's have some champagne." Tina looked around for the waiter.

Sunday, Frank called his parents. He and Lanie both spoke to them. They were surprised but very happy to hear about the engagement. It was decided that they would fly down the end of the following week and spend the weekend getting to know both Lanie and Cassie.

Frank and Lanie set up a family dinner for the following Saturday night. Aside from his parents, they invited Lanie's mother, Tina, Frank's brother and sister, and his sister's family. They also invited Kate and Bob, Jack and Laura and their kids.

They worked like demons to get Frank's new house ready for the dinner party. Only the kitchen, downstairs bath and dining area would be finished inside the house but the playground outside was ready for the kids.

The dinner proved to be fun and frantic. Frank's mother, Grace, was a small woman with a ready smile and good looks that defied anyone who tried to guess her age. She could have been Frank's sister. Frank's father, Ron, was tall and easy-going; a preview of what Frank would look like as he grew older. He was quieter though. Lanie soon decided that Frank had gotten his ready sense of humor from his mother.

Frank's brother summed up his feelings about Lanie with the remark, "It's too bad he saw you first. Do you have a sister?"

"Yes. I do." Lanie smiled and introduced him to Tina, who was only too happy to spend some time with him.

For the actual meal, they went the easy route: pizza and fried chicken, salads, beer and soft drinks. Cooking for a dozen odd adults and assorted kids in a half-finished house didn't sound like a relaxed family get together, it sounded like madness. The weekend was a success; everyone fit together as if they'd been a family for a long time. The date for the wedding was set for approximately three months away, at the end of August.

The next few weeks passed in a frenetic blur as Lanie and

Frank made wedding plans and tried to get the remodeling on his new house finished. They both worked hard on each of those projects. When they had a chance to relax, they sat quietly and talked about their future together.

Lanie worked extra hard, first because she was finishing the landscaping on Frank's new house, their new house, and also because she was helping Frank on the interiors now, making it a warm, loving home for herself, Frank, Cassie and any future children she and Frank might have.

When she thought about having children with Frank, she smiled to herself and her legs went weak. How would it feel, she wondered, to have a baby with a man who wanted the child and who looked forward to the joy of raising it with her? How would it feel to have a husband who would stay by her side and support her? The idea seemed almost too good to be true, especially if that husband was Frank.

Together, they decided to go ahead with almost all of Frank's extensive plans for renovating the old house right away instead of doing it piecemeal as he had originally planned. Somehow it suddenly seemed important to get it ready to be a real home. Frank had to get some extra funding to do the more extensive renovations so quickly but it seemed well worth it, especially when Lanie suggested that they hold the wedding outside their new home as soon as the landscaping was ready. They both stretched their resources pretty slim to get everything done on time but when they worked out a budget, it fit. The saving grace was that as soon as Frank moved into the new house he would stop paying rent on his apartment, and as soon as Lanie moved in Tina would take over her house payments and move into Lanie's old house. Those savings would be enough to get their budget back on track.

After about a month of working on his house and some serious lovemaking in any spot where they could find a comfortable surface and a bit of privacy, things were finally starting to take shape. The newly planted lawn had sprouted. It looked green, plush, and healthy. Some of the plants were starting to grow. Lanie planted the flower beds with colorful plants, already starting to blossom. There were now a wide variety of blossoms in almost every conceivable color. The trees were still saplings, of course, but they looked good. The dwarf fruit trees she'd planted were already full of lemons, limes and oranges.

The area where the pool was going to be was temporarily planted with grass. It would be covered with folding chairs and tables, and the wedding would be held in a white gazebo at the edge of that area. Putting in the pool would be next year's project. Cassie's play area was already complete. There was a sturdy swing set, a slide, places to climb and a large redwood playhouse.

The house had been transformed. The outside was sanded and painted. It now had forest green trim and crisp white paint. The porch had been rebuilt, and a redwood deck led to the future pool area. The roof was also retiled. Inside the house the downstairs rooms: the kitchen, dining room and bathroom, were finished being rebuilt and now fully decorated.

The living areas were opened up into one large airy room. The kitchen had an island between it and the dining room. The dining room opened into the living area which had furniture groupings for conversation, watching TV, reading, an office setting, and a fireplace. Upstairs, most of the major construction was done. The master bedroom was perfect with large walk-in closets, a roomy bathroom, and a sitting area.

Even Cassie's bedroom was finished, along with the second upstairs bath and the other bedroom, which was also decorated as an office, temporarily. There was plenty of room to expand the house if more bedrooms were needed in the future. The sitting room in the master bedroom could also be converted into a nursery. The walls were painted a soft off-white throughout the house, and new fixtures had been installed in the bathrooms.

There were also new appliances in the kitchen.

In an amazingly short period of time, and at considerable extra cost, the major work was done. Soon, there was only the decorating left to do. Lanie and Frank discussed, argued and eventually agreed over furniture, wallpaper, carpets and even knickknacks. Frank left most of the details to Lanie but as usual he enjoyed giving her a hard time.

There was the famous incident when he decided to tell Lanie that he would like to have a moose head on the wall of the family room over the fireplace. He was firmly told that his own head would be mounted there first. Then Lanie casually started getting undressed for bed. Just about the time her bra hit the ground, Frank looked Lanie in the eyes and noticed a glint of anger. He quickly admitted that he didn't like having dead animals mounted on his walls either.

All in all, it was a monumental project to get completed before the wedding. At some points along the way tempers wore thin and arguments over tiny, silly details flared up. They had a doozie over the color of pillowcases, which ended with feathers all over the bedroom and lovemaking on the bedroom floor, not even bothering to get on the bed. It was wonderful.

Lanie almost shoved a cream pie in Frank's face when he told her flatly one day that he wouldn't allow her to put pink towels in the master bath.

"They're not pink, you idiot!" She had the pie in her hands, and for a minute he could see her fighting the temptation. "They're peach, and they look wonderful with the wallpaper and the new ceramic tiles.

"Peach, pink." Frank shrugged and then played with fire by asking, "What's the difference?"

"The difference is that they're a different color." Lanie picked up a knife and cut the pie with a suspiciously vicious slicing motion before asking, "What's wrong with peach?"

"It's too feminine," Frank stated firmly.

Lanie responded to that with a one-word reference to the manure she used for fertilizer.

She calmed herself down and told him gently, "It's a cool, refreshing color." Gradually things were taking shape.

Lanie arrived home one day from working on the new house and saw a man on her doorstep. He looked familiar. She drove closer and felt a shiver run down her spine. It couldn't be but it was. It was Cal!

She slowly got out of the car and reluctantly greeted him. "Hello, Cal, what are you doing here?"

Cal looked at her with a wide smile. He looked almost the same as he had ten years ago. He was still slightly over six-feet tall, his eyes were still a brilliant green, his golden blond hair was still too long, and his body was still fairly firm and well muscled.

The only noticeable changes were some traces of lines around the corners of his eyes, the faint trace of red veins on his nose, and the merest hint of the beginning of a spare tire around his waist. They weren't merely the first signs of aging; they were also the early warning signs of a lifetime of too many women, too much drinking, and too many late nights.

"My parents tell me that you have a daughter, my daughter," he told her after some preliminaries. "I want to see her, Lanie. Please."

Lanie had always believed that if Cal ever grew up emotionally, he would want to get to know his daughter. So for the next two weeks, she let him visit with Cassie and even take her to the zoo and park a few times. Sometimes she even felt a trace of her old attraction for Cal, but it was only a trace, like a vague memory of something long gone. She had a long discussion, more like a fight, about Cal with Frank.

"Of course I have to let him spend some time with Cassie, he's her birth father!" she insisted. "You sound jealous."

"Face it, he was nothing more than a sperm donor," Frank said shortly. "Cassie needs a real father. She needs someone to

love her and to be there for her. Cal will only hurt her. I'm
telling you now: He's here because he wants something, maybe
you, maybe Cassie, but probably money, and if he gets it he'll
suddenly drop out of Cassie's life again. How could I be jealous
of a creep like that?"

"Cal doesn't want me." Lanie was shocked. "I know he
doesn't. He couldn't."

"Why not?" Frank yelled. "You're beautiful, passionate, and
intelligent. He'd have to be an idiot not to want you."

The rising anger drained right out of Lanie. She smiled gently
and said, "I'm glad you think so, my love, but Cal isn't you. He is
an idiot. You're right, I think he has an ulterior motive for all the
attention he's paying to Cassie and I'm forewarned. I won't let
her be hurt by him or anyone else. I just want to find out what
he's after. And Frank, Cassie's not stupid. She doesn't believe
he's here to stay either, she told me she thinks he's a big phony."

Cal had a real easy way with Cassie and outwardly she seemed
to like him well enough, although she never seemed to get truly
close to him like she was to Frank.

After Cal had seen Cassie a few times he finally spoke to
Lanie about her. "I didn't just come back here to get to know the
brat. I want her."

It had happened, he had just exposed his true colors. Any
trace of the old attraction Lanie felt vanished completely, and she
was gloriously mad.

"You can't have her, you idiot." Lanie's eyes flashed. "And
why do you say you want her? You barely even know her name.
It's not brat, it's Cassie. Hell, even your parents have refused to
see her."

"They thought you were just using your pregnancy to try and
get your hands on our family money," Cal offered by way of an
explanation.

"What family money?" Lanie was truly puzzled. "Your
parents are as poor as church mice."

"My grandfather is rich, really rich," Frank told her, "but the old goat doesn't think much of my folks or of me either, for that matter. He always complains that I never grew up. He wants me to stop drinking and settle down. He thinks I should get a job, get married and become what he calls respectable. I think he might put me in his will if I followed his advice and got married and had a family. He seemed to hint at it when I went to him last month to ask him for a small loan."

"You want me to marry you?" Lanie was incredulous. "You must be nuts!"

"Of course not, why the hell would I marry you?" Cal looked her over contemptuously then laughed heartily. "I have a girlfriend, Doreen. She makes you look like a boy."

"Then make a baby with Doreen and leave Cassie and me alone," Lanie ordered.

"Doreen can't have children," Cal admitted, "she's infertile."

"Then adopt or find another girlfriend, but you will never get your hands on Cassie," Lanie told him. "In fact, I want you to sign over your rights to Cassie so that my fiancé, Frank, can adopt her."

"Of course if you wanted, I guess we could get married," Cal suggested as though he hadn't heard Lanie. "That way, I could share some of the old goat's money with you, and you could help me take care of Cassie. Of course both of us could keep our real lovers on the side."

"Get off my land, you disgust me." Lanie shuttered. "When I realize that you're Cassie's father, I feel ill."

"I'll let you think it over. In fact I'll give you a whole month to decide, and then I'll sue you for custody," Cal threatened. "And I'll win."

"Fine. I'll see you in court." Lanie turned her back on him mainly to stop him from seeing the anger in her eyes. After Cal left she sat down on the steps.

Tina came over to find Lanie sitting on the doorstep, clearly agitated.

"What's up, Sis?" Tina asked.

Lanie told her about the demands Cal had made. "The creep. He claims I hid his daughter from him, that I denied him the joy of knowing her, and refused him his parental rights. He wants us to get back together so that we can raise Cassie as a real family or else he'll sue for custody claiming I never told him he had a daughter. Of course, we each get to keep our lovers."

"Do you think he means it?" Tina asked.

"Sure, in his own twisted way. He means to harass me and make it difficult for me to get married, that's why he picked a one month deadline since my wedding is six weeks away. I suspect that he wants me to pay him off to make up for what he thinks he might inherit from his grandfather. Then maybe he'll consider surrendering his parental rights to Cassie and letting Frank adopt her."

"The strange thing is, I didn't even know that he knew you'd had the baby, let alone that you'd had a girl. I just thought he'd figured that you would have given in to his demands and had the abortion, especially when he'd left you high and dry," Tina said. "How did he find out that you'd gone through with the pregnancy?"

"Even rats have parents. Parent rats. I can't understand why Cassie's paternal grandparents have never even asked to see or meet Cassie, much less sent her a birthday card or a gift. They must have seen her around town with me but they've never even walked over to say hello to either of us." Lanie had worried about Cal's family for a long time. "Somehow, I always knew that if they thought they had anything to gain from Cassie they'd turn up with their hands out."

"So what are you going to do?" Tina worried.

"I'm not the scared teenager I was when Cal and I were together," Lanie reminded her. "I've changed, I've grown up. Now I fight. I'm going to hire a lawyer and get all the proof I can that he abandoned me and surrendered his parental rights long ago, and I'm going to fight. I plan to sue him for nine years of back child support. The only way I will surrender my right to the back child support he owes me--is if he allows Cassie to be adopted by Frank. But there's one thing I want to try first."

"What's that?" Even Tina was impressed by the determination in Lanie's eyes.

"I'm going to try scaring him off," Lanie grinned, "and let him know just how much I've changed since we were together."

"How?" Tina knew there would be a plan.

"You'll see." Lanie kept grinning. "Just wait and you'll see."

The next day she met with Frank and one of his co-workers, a man named John Wilson, head of the Loss Prevention department of the company that Frank worked for. John was a tall, good-looking black man. Together the three of them formulated a plan. Almost three weeks later she called Cal and invited him over for a special dinner. As she issued the invitation she told him it was time to talk. Cal was only too happy to accept.

He took the bait just like a rat takes the cheese, Lanie thought. When he arrived that night Lanie opened the door and he walked in. Snap!

Chapter Seventeen

"So?" Cal asked as soon as he entered Lanie's house. "Have you used your pea-brain and thought about what you're going to do? Are you going to give in and marry me or will you just give me outright custody of Cassie? Those are your only choices because I know you're not going to put up a fight. You don't have the guts to stand up to me."

Lanie noted that he had dressed up for the occasion. For once he'd shed his usual faded jeans and torn t-shirt for pressed black trousers and a pin-striped shirt with a sedate print tie. He'd evidently left his tact at home, however, if he had any.

His arrogance astounded Lanie but she struggled to keep her cool. "Cal, this isn't easy for me. We need to talk more before I give you my final decision. Let's relax and eat our dinner before we have this discussion," Lanie told him, forcing a smile.

Her struggle to hold her temper in and her nervousness made her seem to be the timid creature Cal expected. It was a false impression.

Despite his preference for casual attire, Cal was a real stickler for having good food and a nicely set table at dinner, as long as he didn't have to do the cooking or set the table. Lanie, knowing this, had put extra effort into the dinner. She had fixed his favorite meal: spaghetti, garlic bread, a fresh salad, and red wine.

The table was just how he liked it, the good china, Lanie's best crystal, the candles lit, and the flatware shining. She had made a floral centerpiece. Lanie herself was in a black dress with a modest neckline, and her hair was piled high on top of her head. Cassie was staying with Tina for the evening. The funny thing was however, Cal never even asked where Cassie, the little girl he claimed to want so much, was.

After dinner, Lanie and Cal sat side by side on the living room sofa and sipped the rest of their wine. Lanie was tense, every nerve stretched to the breaking point, waiting for Cal to make his move. She tried to keep Frank and John's instructions firmly in her mind.

Finally, sounding impatient, Cal repeated the same question he'd asked when Lanie had opened the door. "Well, is it marriage or will you just give me custody of the girl? I won't even ask you for child support." He sneered, "At least, not much child support."

"You want me to pay you for taking my child away!" Lanie's temper flared, but with tremendous effort she reined it in. Her obvious reluctance to get angry with Cal only reinforced his mental image of her as being a cowed victim. "You've never paid me any child support at all and your daughter is nine years old!" Lanie was indignant. "If you took Cassie away from me right now, I could still sue you for the back child support and interest."

"So giving me custody is out, it's marriage then?" Cal prodded, ignoring her outburst.

"How can I come back to you? Marry you?" Lanie retorted bitterly. "I wasn't the one who left in the first place. You did. I would have stayed with you no matter how abusive you were because I thought I loved you. You don't know how hard it was going on without you, going through the pregnancy without you. I had to face childbirth alone."

"So what?" Cal snorted, "What's the big deal about that? Women have babies all the time."

"You see?" Lanie was getting frustrated. "You just don't get it. I needed you and you weren't there. That's why I had to find someone else. I needed someone's love and support."

"You're just like me then, for all your protests; all you're after is someone else to support you," Cal gloated. "And you have the nerve to act so smug and superior."

"Emotional support, you idiot, I pay my own way with money I've earned myself. I work hard and I always have. I can prove that in court if I have to." She enunciated slowly, as if she was speaking to an idiot, "I wanted someone to give me the love and emotional support I needed."

Lanie glossed over the fact that it had taken her nine years to find that someone. She skipped the details that she had, in fact, gone on without him and proved herself successful. She had paid the hospital bills when Cassie was born. She had completed her education and made a career for herself. She was a full partner in her own business. She had bought a house and made it into a home for Cassie and herself. She looked at Cal silently and realized just how shallow his shell was.

"So are you going to give me Cassie?" He pushed, "Or do I have to take you to court?"

"Why should I give her to you? What's in it for Cassie? What's in it for me?" Her chin raised, she tried to meet greed with greed. "She's mine. She's the best thing that's ever happened to me. She's my angel. She's the only truly good thing that ever came out of my relationship with a pathetic loser like you." Inside her stomach twisted in agony as she uttered these words. "She's so sweet and loving, it's hard to believe there's any of your blood in her veins."

"You're going to give her to me because I need her to get any inheritance from my grandfather," Cal shot back. "The old coot doesn't think much of me, he even said that I should just work for a living like everyone else. But if I get married and give him a grandchild, he'll come around, especially if she's as lovable as you say she is."

"That's your problem," Lanie said coldly, her act completely forgotten, "what has it got to do with me? I don't even know your grandfather but he sounds like he has good judgment. Besides, you don't love Cassie; you don't even know her, not really. I'll bet that if you saw her on a playground full of little girls you couldn't even pick her out from the crowd. You just want to use her for your personal gain. That's the difference between us, Cal. I love Cassie. I really love her. I'll never give her up."

"So why don't you and I just get married, that way we'll both have Cassie? I can still have Doreen on the side and you can have this guy you claim you're in love with, whoever he is." Cal leered at her. "Who knows? Maybe once in a while, I can take care of you, too. In bed. You're not as sexy as Doreen is but if I remember right, you're not too bad in the sack." Cal started to stroke Lanie's cheek.

"Cal, don't even think it!" Lanie slid away from him, pushing against the side of the sofa. "Don't you ever touch me again."

"Babe, I can make you so hot for me, just like I did when you were a teenager." Cal followed her using the end of the sofa to trap her, leaning over her to force a kiss on her. One of his hands was grabbing at the neckline of her dress. She slapped him across the face, hard. "In fact, you want me. That's why you had everything so perfect here tonight."

"I do not want you," Lanie said clearly. "The thought makes me sick to my stomach."

"I can change your mind, I always could." He sneered.

Suddenly he got nasty, really nasty. Even knowing that she was not really alone with Cal, a chill of panic ran through Lanie. He had been an abusive bully when they were young, and now she realized that he had never grown up at all. His passion could turn to rage in an instant.

He was the type of man who would rape a woman, leaving her bruised and battered, then boast to his friends and claim that he had only given her what she wanted. Deep inside his twisted mind he might even really believe it, and that was truly frightening.

Lanie had learned a few tricks in the intervening years, however. Even as he ripped at her clothes she fought back, scratching his face before her knee found a vital spot between his legs. When he doubled over in pain, she scrambled off the sofa and dug her can of pepper spray out of her purse. She stood her ground with him, the nozzle aimed directly at his face, and then let him have it.

"I'll never let you have Cassie." In her anger she practically screamed at him as Cal cried out and covered his eyes with his hands. "In fact, I'll never let you see her again."

"Then I'll take her." Cal's voice was strained but was still threatening, even with tears streaming down his face. "I'll sue for custody and claim that you refused to let me have any visitation with her, and of course, that you're an unfit mother."

"Unfit? Compared to an abusive bully like you? Compared to a man who refused to be there when I was pregnant? A man who said he was out of there if I didn't have an abortion? A man who never even called to ask me how the pregnancy ended? Much less ever paid one penny of support? How, just exactly how do you think you can do that?" Lanie tried to control her breathing. "You're not even a father; you're just a sperm donor."

"First, you lied to me and told me you had aborted my baby," Cal said snidely.

"That's not true!" Lanie shouted. "I told you I would never abort."

"Who cares? It'll be your word against mine in court. My parents will back me up." Cal sneered. "Besides that, you're carrying on with several men around town and you drink way too much. I can get witnesses. I already have some. My parents have said they will testify that you lied about the abortion, and some of my old friends will swear they've slept and partied with you. They'll say whatever I want them to." Cal smiled wickedly. "Hell, I'll even find a way to plant some marijuana somewhere in one of your nurseries or groves. You'd never know where or when. Then I'll make an anonymous tip to the police and voila! You'd have a record for using, maybe even dealing drugs. Heck, it'd be real easy."

"And just how will you prove that I refused to give you visitation with Cassie?" she asked.

"Hell, even the kid can say that she never saw me until she was nine," Cal jeered, "and I can make sure she likes me, enough toys and candy will take care of that. She only has your word for it that we never met because I never wanted to see her."

"What if all that doesn't work?" Lanie prodded, fighting the urge to use the pepper spray on him again. "What then?"

"If I have to, I'll just take her and we'll disappear." Cal bragged, "You'll never find either one of us."

"If you ever take her, I will hunt you to the ends of the earth and I will kill you," Lanie whispered, her throat tight. "I swear it."

"And if you did, that would cost you custody of Cassie forever," Cal taunted her.

"But at least she wouldn't be with you!" Lanie's blood ran cold. "I'd rather face a lifetime in prison than let you have her."

Feigning a calm she could not possibly feel, she said in a steady voice, "Cal, I have to think about this a bit longer, so please leave." She quickly hustled him out of her house.

No sooner had he left than Frank and John came in her back door. Suddenly shaking, Lanie turned to Frank. He wrapped her in a bear hug, murmuring to her while she sobbed. John walked over to the video camera he had hidden on Lanie's crowded bookshelf and pulled out the videotape. Hooking his VCR up to Lanie's, they all watched the tape while John made a duplicate.

"I'll kill him!" Frank said as he saw the end of the tape.

"You don't have to, we got him!" John was confident. "He's said everything we need. He admitted that he knew and didn't care that Lanie never had an abortion. He admitted he never supported Cassie. He said that he only wanted Cassie to help him get an inheritance from his grandfather so that he wouldn't have to work for a living. He threatened Lanie and listed how he could frame her in court with false witnesses and planted evidence. He also threatened to kidnap Cassie. He's on record for all of it."

"I threatened him, too," Lanie admitted. "That's on the tape."

"But only in defense of Cassie," John said, "no one will criticize you for that, in fact they'll cheer you on. The difference between his threats and yours come across clearly on the video."

"He really scares me," Lanie admitted. "What if he still tries to take Cassie?"

"He only wants her for the money. If we use the tape wisely we can eliminate the profit motive, and in turn the threat. We have to find a way to do it without pushing him to act out of anger or revenge." John was thinking even as he spoke. "And, of course, we can have him charged with sexual assault."

"Will the tape stand up in court?" Frank asked.

"Probably not. I'm not sure. Case law is weird," John explained, "since the tape was made without Cal's knowledge or consent but it may be possible to use it to impeach his witnesses. We can definitely use it to let the police know about his threats, especially the threat to take Cassie."

"So?" Lanie asked. "What do we do next?"

"We press charges. Then we make enough copies of this tape to send a copy to Cal, his parents, his lawyers, our lawyers, and to his rich grandfather. We show a copy to the police. And we keep the original safely in a bank vault," John explained. "Of course we'll install a security system in your house and also put some protection around both you and Cassie at least until he gives up and provides his consent for Frank to adopt Cassie."

"Won't he be too mad to do that?" Frank asked. "He'll withhold consent for revenge."

"He's going broke," John countered. "That fancy, uh, girlfriend of his is taking up all of his money and when it's gone, she'll be gone too."

"So we offer him a pay-off," Frank finished for John. "How much will it take?"

"First we sue him for back support then, if we have to, we offer to drop the claim and, as a last resort, we might even give him a little money. I wouldn't go over five thousand. *If* that." John suggested, "Let me handle this part of it, okay? I'm not emotionally involved." The anger showing in his face made this a blatant lie.

"Thanks, John." Lanie was grateful as she kissed him on the cheek. "I really appreciate this."

"It's a change from catching shoplifters." John started to leave then turned back at the door. "Want to hear what we turned up on Cal's girlfriend, Doreen? You might like it." He grinned. "I don't think Cal knows this, but Doreen used to be Donald. That's why she can't have any kids. My operative says she's even nice, in a money-grubbing way. He doesn't think she's in on Cal's scheme. He also doesn't think she'll stay with Cal if she finds out how he's treating you. She's pretty, too." John showed them a picture of what appeared to be a very pretty showgirl.

"Sounds like your man likes her." Frank smiled.

"In a funny way he did, for a while." John smiled. "Poor guy was having a real sexual identity crises over it."

"What happened?" Frank asked, amused.

"Kate and Laura introduced him to someone, of course." John smiled broadly. "Just like they did with you two, and Cheryl and me. His identity crises faded instantly. His wedding is about a month after yours."

"He'll be happy then." Lanie smiled.

"Delirious." John smiled. "And if Doreen turns on Cal and leaves him when she finds out what he's really like, I wouldn't put it past Kate and Laurie to find someone for her."

John pulled on a coat and left. As soon as he was out the door Frank took Lanie's hand and led her upstairs.

The recorded videotapes brought a variety of reactions. Cal

was blindingly furious but he had learned his lesson. He had enough brains not to threaten Lanie, barely enough brains. Lanie taped the phone call he made in response to the tape, and she told him she taped it to make sure it was legal.

Cal's parents sent Lanie a polite letter disclaiming his actions but they still made no request to see Cassie. Even Doreen, Cal's so-called girlfriend, called Lanie. She was very pleasant and very apologetic for Cal. Doreen told Lanie that Cal had mentioned to her that Lanie was a bad mother and that Cal had battled for years to get custody of Cassie. She admitted that the tape had convinced her otherwise, and let Lanie know that she would testify in court if she had any information that would help Lanie's case. Doreen said she was breaking up with Cal and had finally realized the kind of man her really was.

Lanie's attorney easily received a protective order against Cal and he also began proceedings to collect back child support. This action brought an additional outcry from both Cal and his parents.

The most surprising reaction to the tape came from Cal's grandfather. He called Lanie and asked if he could come over for a visit. Lanie was touched by the sincere tone in the old man's voice and agreed, but she had the camera set up and running just in case. Frank was at her side as she greeted Cassie's great-grandfather at the door.

"Hello, Ms. McPherson, I'm Michael Westingham," he greeted her as he held out his hand. "Please call me Michael."

"Please come in Michael, I'm Lanie and this is Frank, my fiancé. It's good to meet you."

The elderly gentleman allowed himself to be led inside and accepted a cup of tea before the conversation continued. "I feel I must apologize for my grandson, Cal, and even for his parents. Instead of appreciating your daughter, Cassie, in her own right as she deserved, they saw her as a means to use for their own personal gain. That's sad and shocking," Michael said. "I can never make up for all that Cal made you suffer but I can make sure that he never bothers you again. I have deeded over to him a small ranch I own in Montana. I have also arranged for him to receive an annual allowance if he signs over adoption rights to Frank. If he can make a go of the ranch, he will be set for life, but it definitely will not be easy. He'll have a tight budget and some extremely hard work to do. Not to mention some of the harshest winter weather known to man to overcome. I've put a codicil in my will that if he ever contacts you or Cassie again he will lose the annual allowance. His parents are cut out of my will except for a small remembrance. I'm leaving my estate to Cassie, in a trust, with the provision for it to be split at your discretion between any half-brothers and sisters you might give her. All I ask is that I can visit her from time to time."

"There are two provisions that I would like before I agree to let you visit Cassie," Lanie said softly. "First, if you start visiting her, keep visiting her, don't let her begin to care for you and then disappear from her life. Also, if we have other kids, treat them the same as you do Cassie. I know she'll be the only one who's your real blood but I want you to treat any children we have with equal care and love, no playing favorites, agreed?"

Michael nodded. "Of course."

"As for seeing Cassie, I'm sure she would like that but it's up to her. Would you like to meet her?" At his speechless nod, Lanie left the room and returned with Cassie.

The older man and the little girl had a long talk.

Afterwards when he left Lanie asked her daughter, "How did you like him?"

"He was very nice," Cassie said, "but he seemed very sad. Did I cause him to be sad?"

"No Sweetie," Lanie told her gently, "he's sad because he has realized that his grandson, Cal, is not a nice man. He liked you. Cassie, do you know what a great-grandfather is?"

"Yes," she said with mounting excitement, "is he my great-grandfather?"

"Yes he is," Lanie smiled at Cassie, "would you like him to visit you from time to time?"

"Of course," Cassie said simply, "why not?"

Chapter Eighteen

For the next couple of weeks, both Frank and Lanie were extremely busy attending to the thousands of tiny never-ending details involved in putting on a wedding, especially within just three short months. There was one other detail they had to attend to: about a month after Lanie's confrontation with Cal, Lanie received his approval to have Frank adopt Cassie. They immediately went to their lawyer to set things in motion.

They also picked out wedding invitations and argued over the guest list, then spent several evenings addressing the envelopes. Cassie was in charge of stamps. They hired a caterer but only after they had tasted food at every catering company they could think of and then argued about the menu and the cost. They decided on a buffet with hand-carved ham and roast beef, some casseroles, plus several salads and side dishes. They also decided to have an open bar.

Then Lanie dragged Frank all over creation to search for the perfect wedding cake. She wanted a traditional white cake but with a tart lemon filling. Of course it had to be four-tiered and decorated perfectly. She chose a cake that was completely covered with very realistic looking roses made from frosting so that not an inch of the cake seemed to have been covered with just plain icing. Of course, Lanie used her own influence with various growers to get plenty of flowers. Frank took charge of finding a live band for the reception.

Not only did they have the usual wedding details to attend to as well as filing adoption papers, but they also had the house and the surrounding grounds to complete and get ready. Luckily the construction on the house and basic work in the yard were both finished in an amazingly short amount of time. Frank had pulled every string he could to get the work done on time including paying a few cash incentives to some of the construction workers, and even picked up a hammer himself when his busy schedule permitted.

Although it was a bit unusual, the house was furnished room by room as soon as the construction crews finished in an area. Frank and Lanie spent several long evenings searching the furniture stores, plus selected carpeting, wallpaper, window treatments, and paint shades. They fought and pleaded with storeowners to hold furniture and have it delivered as soon as the room was painted, papered, and carpeted.

Soon, the furnished house was looking wonderful and warm, a home any family would be happy to live and grow in. The only thing missing were the signs of everyday life and the normal mess that comes from living in a home because neither Frank nor Lanie had moved in yet; they had both decided to live in their old homes until the wedding. As a result, the house still seemed like a model home, just a bit too organized and sterile to be a real home.

Both of them had, however, moved everything to the new house except a few clothes, grooming items, and the things they planned to take with them on their honeymoon. Frank's apartment was already rented to someone new who would move in on the Monday after the wedding. Tina was renting Lanie's little house from her, taking over Lanie's house payments. She was even considering buying it for herself from Lanie.

Kate and Laura threw a Bridal Shower for Lanie. Her mother, Tina, and Cassie came, as did Frank's mother. His sister Linda and her two daughters who were eight and nine drove down from their home in Bakersfield too. They stayed with Lanie for the weekend and Cassie took great pride in showing them around Disneyland the day after the wedding shower. The trio of girls walked their legs off, dragging a slightly hung over

Aunt Tina and Cassie's soon-to-be Aunt Linda with them. Of course, several of Lanie's other friends were also there.

It had been planned for everyone to bring two presents: One was to be a normal practical wedding gift such as the usual toaster or blender, the other was to be lingerie, the sexier the better. The women gossiped, laughed a lot, plotted to get Tina married next, and drank champagne punch. After sending the kids off to a kiddie movie with what they called 'the men folk', the women had a male stripper dance for them.

They had taken great care in hiring him, with Tina volunteering for the arduous duty of picking the stripper. He could really dance well but his act was tasteful and fun, not sleazy. Out of respect for Lanie and Frank's mothers and some of the older guests, he didn't strip down to the all-together. Lanie and Tina might have been surprised to find out that some of those same women were a bit disappointed about that. The men folk provided taxi service, driving home any party guest who had a bit too much of the really delicious champagne punch.

Naturally, Jack and Bob held a bachelor party for Frank. Similarly it was also tasteful and fun, but not excessively vulgar. Jack and Bob knew exactly how far they could let things go. They had a stripper, but no prostitutes. There was drinking but no one drove home drunk. Jack and Bob both knew their lives would be over if they let things get too far out of hand.

Lanie and Frank slept apart the whole week before the wedding, a symbolic gesture to separate their married life from their single lives. It also had the side effect of making them anticipate the honeymoon even more than before. The passion between them was hot and the anticipation was delicious.

Frank's parents came down from Oregon about two weeks before the wedding to help with any last minute details and to really have a chance to visit. Lanie had already fallen in love with the Morgans. They had both fallen in love with her and Cassie instantly at the engagement party and now declared that Cassie was an official Morgan granddaughter, and a welcome bonus addition to the family. A few days before the actual wedding, Frank's older sister Linda and her family drove down from Bakersfield, and his younger brother Ted, also flew down from San Francisco.

During the week before the wedding Frank's sister worked on Lanie's hair, practicing several styles. She told Lanie, "Watch out for my brother. Don't let him get away with anything. Oh, I don't mean women, I know he'll be faithful to you. I can tell he really loves you. I mean his pranks and his orneriness. He can be such a pain in the patooty. Keep him in line."

"Don't worry, I will," Lanie promised solemnly, but with a grin on her face. "He's easy to handle once you know how."

Frank picked Lanie up at her office about three days before the wedding. Unbeknownst to Lanie, he had a surprise for Cassie that he wanted to receive Lanie's approval on beforehand. Frank had his eye on a very special wedding gift for Cassie, or an adoption gift, whichever was the easiest to get Lanie's blessing.

Without telling Lanie where they were going, he drove her out towards the desert. Shortly after crossing the El Cajon pass, he pulled off the main highway and soon pulled to a stop in front of a small house on a large lot.

"What are we here for?" Lanie was curious.

Frank looked distinctly uncomfortable. "I know I need your permission to do this, Lanie, but I'd like to get Cassie a very special gift to let her know how proud I'll be to have her for my daughter." He opened the door for her and hand in hand they went up to knock on the front door of the house.

"Frank! I was hoping you'd come out," a woman greeted him warmly. "And this must be Lanie. Hi, I'm Alice. I've heard about you. I hope you'll be very happy, Frank's a good guy." She turned back to Frank. "Buddy's all ready for you out back. I'd go out with you but I'm babysitting my grandson and the baby's fussy. Don had to work late. You know where everything is."

"I sure do." Frank took Lanie's hand and led her behind the house. "You go take care of that grandbaby, we'll be in later. Wish me luck."

Lanie followed, puzzled and excited; it was very apparent that Frank was eager to show her his surprise. As soon as they rounded the side of the house he left her standing in the yard for a moment. Lanie gasped as he returned with his surprise in tow.

He'd picked out a horse to buy for Cassie. Once Lanie found out what the surprise was all about, the horse became the subject of an intense discussion.

"Frank! A horse is a big monthly expense, and Cassie doesn't know how to ride well enough to get her own horse!" Lanie protested.

"I know, but it was too good a deal to pass up." Frank explained, "I know the people selling this horse, Don and Alice. His name is Buddy. He belonged to their eldest daughter who's leaving for college. The horse is very gentle and well trained. I've ridden him myself many times. He's also very healthy; I've had him vet checked." Frank grinned and gestured at the horse he'd just tied to the fence. "Heck, he's even a fine-looking animal with good conformation. As you can see, he's sorrel with a flaxen mane and tail." Frank paused. "The thing was, because he's a fairly small horse and fifteen years old, the only buyers they had found so far were meat companies. They called me on a whim without knowing about Cassie. It seemed like fate. Lanie, I know this horse, he's like a friend of mine, I couldn't let them--"

"Can you teach Cassie to ride him?" Lanie asked quietly, understanding now. "I mean the fine points."

"Sure." Frank grinned as he saddled the horse. "And remember, she'll learn faster on her own horse because she'll know his quirks and he'll know hers. I also thought I'd get her some professional lessons if she decides she wants to show him.

He's been shown a lot in Western Pleasure and Trail classes."

"Can I ride him?" Lanie laughed, won over. "I know I'm going to say yes but I should at least try him out, just to save face."

"You can ride him this time but once I give him to Cassie, then--" he grinned, "well, then you can ride him only if Cassie lets you." Frank kissed her nose. "He's for her."

Lanie mounted Buddy and rode him around the small pen. She noted that he had a soft mouth, smooth gaits and very good manners. He seemed calm and reliable. He was a pleasure to ride. It was as simple as that, the gelding had a new home; his new owners were very happy and his former owners were very relieved.

Lanie's mother, Jean, flew in from Arizona. She got on famously with Frank's whole family. She was wonderfully ecstatic about the wedding but had one problem: she'd gone out shopping for days to find the perfect dress for the occasion and she still wasn't satisfied. She kidnapped Frank's mother and the two women drove up to an exclusive mall, still looking for the perfect dresses. Lanie shook her head thinking of it, the last person she had expected to get obsessed with a dress was her mother. Jean was usually happiest digging in the dirt and working with plants.

Lanie had no idea just how excited and happy her mother was about the wedding. Jean's deepest dream was to find a good husband for both of her daughters and, of course, to have some more grandchildren. She was so happy that she constantly seemed about to burst into song.

However she wasn't so happy that she failed to take notice of the signs of romance between Frank's brother Ted and Tina. Secretly she hoped Lanie and Frank's romance could lead to a second one. How else could she be sure she'd like the in-laws? The Morgans were perfect.

Both families helped with the last minute details and got to know the respective new relatives. Luckily for Frank and Lanie everyone soon became thick as thieves.

The day before the wedding hundreds of flowers were delivered to the house, along with white wooden folding chairs, tables, and a tent. It was chaos but everything was set up and ready by one o'clock in the afternoon, and it was a darn good thing because they had plans for later that afternoon, big plans.

That was the time set aside for the wedding rehearsal. It went off perfectly with Tina acting as the Maid of Honor, and Frank's sister, Kate, Laura and Cassie acting as attendants. Cassie was proud to be in the wedding, and especially proud to be not just a flower girl but a real Bridesmaid. Frank's brother was Best Man, Bob and Jack were Groomsmen along with the son of one of Frank's friends who was drafted to escort Cassie. The young man was a very mature eleven-year-old who was more than happy and willing to pair up with Cassie. He just wasn't too thrilled about wearing a fancy suit, but the promise of a great dinner and wedding cake lured him.

After the rehearsal the whole group went to a local restaurant for the rehearsal dinner. The evening was wonderful with a special dinner of prime rib and cheesecake for dessert. There was lots of racy teasing, raucous laughter, ribald toasts, and loving friends and family.

The next morning brought the delivery of mass quantities of food. The wedding cake was also delivered, but the icing was smeared so the cake decorator quickly got busy in the kitchen making a few quick repairs. A band was set up next to the gazebo. Around noon, guests and gifts began to arrive. Soon, it was time for the wedding.

The wedding day had dawned bright and clear, a slight breeze cooling the autumn heat. Ignoring old customs and superstitions, Frank picked Lanie up at her old house and drove her to their new one. She would get dressed for the ceremony in the newly furnished master bedroom surrounded by giggling and weeping women, while he planned to dress in the room that would soon be Cassie's bedroom.

As a wedding gift Frank bought Lanie a new car, a red four-door with a CD player and all the latest bell and whistles. Lanie bought him a fancy laptop computer that would download into their home PC. Cassie had a gift for her new father too. She bought him a coffee cup saying, "World's greatest DAD." Nothing he's ever received touched Frank more. Cassie bought Lanie a matching cup. Buddy was still a surprise.

The only other surprise gift was a real shock.

Kate brought Oreo to them with a big silver ribbon tied in a bow around her neck and her American Kennel Club papers in a fancy envelope. Kate explained that since the girl who had planned to take Oreo had changed her mind, Oreo needed a new home. So Kate decided that what Lanie and Frank really needed to make their lives together complete was a halfway housebroken Boston Terrier puppy. She handed the little dog to Cassie and kissed the puppy's head.

"You'd better take care of her, Cassie, your mom's awfully busy today. I get the pick of her first litter if you breed her." She told Lanie in an aside, "And Charger and Teddy will be only too happy to give me another little girl."

"Wow!" Lanie teased Frank, "Our family's growing already. Somehow I thought it would take at least nine months."

"So did I," Frank replied, watching Cassie kiss and cuddle the puppy. "But look at Cassie with Oreo. Could anything be more precious?"

"Only the look in your eyes as you look at the two of them." Lanie kissed him gently. "I have to go get dressed."

Lanie went in and dressed. Her attendants were dressed in soft rose colored dresses with capped sleeves, V-necks, and flowing skirts. The bouquets were all shades of rose from the palest pink to the deepest red.

Both Lanie's mother and Frank's were dressed in a deeper

shade of rose, although the dresses they had selected were very different. Jean was in a rose lace dress with a high-collared neck and long sleeves that looked old fashioned and romantic. Frank's mother was in a dress that looked like the finest linen with a swirling skirt and a rounded neckline. Both women looked stunning, very proud, and of course, excited.

The guests were finally seated and waiting for the wedding to begin. The groom's mother and father were seated, followed by the bride's mother. The groomsmen lined up near the gazebo. It was finally time.

Kate's daughters acted as flower girls; they were more experienced now after being the flower girls at Kate's wedding, but they still pelted the guests with the flower petals. Kate's son acted as the ring bearer. The Bridesmaids and Maid of Honor walked slowly down the aisle, meeting up with the Groomsmen in front of the gazebo. The wiggling puppy in Cassie's arms, along with a bouquet, only added a touch of whimsy to the picture. The guests shifted restlessly and waited for the bride to appear. Lanie paused at the end of the aisle as the band started playing the wedding march and Frank's jaw dropped in amazement.

Lanie had indeed saved the copy of her white linen dress for another time. She was wearing it as a wedding dress. She had taken the dress to a seamstress and had filmy lace spotted with tiny fresh water pearls added over the deep v-neck. A beaded choker collar had also been added to the dress, along with a bolero cut jacket. All of the newly added parts of the dress were covered with beads and seed pearls. It was stunning.

The wedding went off without a hitch. It was a beautiful and touching ceremony. Both the bride and groom seemed eager and confident as they stated their vows.

The reception was wonderful. Only a short but loud discussion between Kate and Laura broke into the day. They were both claiming credit for a successful match. The discussion ended when Frank gave both of them credit and reminded Kate that he'd won the bet. Frank and Lanie were going on a four-day honeymoon, then coming back to collect Cassie for a week in San Diego, visiting the San Diego Zoo, Sea World and the Wild Animal Park. While they were in San Diego, the yard would be fenced for Oreo, and a small shed and corral would be built for Buddy. Although it nearly killed both Frank and Lanie to keep the secret, Cassie didn't know about him yet. He was to be delivered the day they returned from San Diego.

"Do you realize something?" Lanie teased her new husband during the reception.

"What?" Frank asked, knowing by the twinkle in her eyes that he was walking into a trap.

"You haven't spilled anything on me, gotten me all muddy, or been locked with me in a musty, dusty basement since the first time we slept together. I'm glad it turned out that you were only, um, horny and that you're not really a total klutz, but I'd love you anyway." She kissed him.

"It's hard to be well coordinated when love knocks you off your feet. Lanie love, you really threw me for a loop." Frank looked around the room and asked, "How long before we can leave this party and be alone?"

"I thought you'd never ask." She grinned, grabbing his hand. "Let's get out of here."

They tried, but the photographer caught them and insisted on taking the traditional shots. Lanie threw her bouquet, Frank threw the garter. They danced with every member of the family, cut the cake, and disappointed everyone by not smearing it all over each other's faces.

"Now can we escape?" Lanie asked plaintively.

"Yes," Frank said assertively, "I dare anyone to try and stop us now."

They slipped out of the reception as though they were involved in a dangerous prison escape, trying to appear casual as they strolled towards Frank's rented limo. Their sneaking around was much to the amusement of all the guests who were watching them, without seeming to. Frank and Lanie didn't realize at first that everyone was watching them so closely. They recognized it when all the guests surrounded the limo and pelted the couple with wild birdseed as they got into the limo.

"Why birdseed?" Frank whispered.

"Because, according to my mom, it's better than rice. You don't have to sweep it up, and even the birds get a treat in honor of your wedding."

"Works for me." Frank pushed the button to slide up the privacy glass and pulled her into his arms. "I want everyone to be as happy as we are right now, even the birds and bees."

"Speaking of the birds and bees--" Lanie reached out and pulled down his zipper.

Epilogue

Did they live happily ever after? Not in quite the way lovers do in fairytales, but they had an active home life full of fun, family and fights. Frank never spilled anything on Lanie again. Well, except for a couple of notable occasions:

It happened every time Lanie told him she was pregnant, and every time she went into labor. With three sons and two daughters, plus two false labors, it only added up to an even dozen ruined outfits. Lanie didn't mind the mess at all.

Lanie and Frank always stood together, either toe to toe when they argued, face to face when they made up, or side by side when they faced off against the rest of the world. They never backed down or left each other's side.

Neither did Cassie, her brothers and sisters, the three dogs, two cats, or the gentle old horse and his two young spirited stable mates. They fought each other and then stood together against all outsiders because that's what families are for.

Isn't it?

Other books by Susan Kohler

The Paddle Club

Hot Crossed Buns

Another Batch of Warm Buns

The Heart of The Beast

Working Romance

Coming soon...

Waiting for Tomorrow